Shad

The Portuguese slavers ca..... ....because they couldn't pronounce his real name. They tore him away from his homeland and put him to work picking cotton in the Tennessee Valley. But the big, fleet-footed Zulu was nobody's slave, and to prove it he escaped and headed west.

Throwing in with a medicine show conman named Doc Jonah, Sam started entering county footraces to earn enough money to go back to Africa. But then his trail crossed that of Major Lawrence Devlin, and nothing was going to stop the ruthless rancher's man from winning the Fort Stockton Carnival Week race.

From that moment forward Sam was cheated, beaten, shot and hunted like an animal. Worse, they took his beautiful grullo mare, U-Shee-nah, away from him. But that was Devlin's biggest mistake, because it only made Sam more determined to get his revenge … and as Shadow Horse he became Devlin's worst nightmare.

By the same authors

STEVE HAYES
AND
BEN BRIDGES

SHADOW HORSE

SIXGOLD

BOOK ENDS

2014

For Woody Strode, Red Skelton and what might have been

Chapter One

The spear slammed into the red Texas dirt barely two inches from its target—a lone cottontail rabbit munching on sunbaked grass along the bank of a shallow river.

Startled, the cottontail immediately bolted for some nearby scrub. With a curse, the man known as Zulu Sam broke cover and sprinted after it.

By any stretch he was an unusual sight. In his early twenties he was lean but muscular, easily six feet in height, with a broad chest, narrow hips and long legs. He was naked save for a deerskin breechclout, a copper armlet and an *isi-coco*—a bone head-ring—set around his shaven head.

Beneath skin the color of burnt umber, his toned muscles worked in perfect precision. Each leaping stride appeared effortless. Though running at great speed he never appeared winded. And not once did he take his eyes—an arresting mixture of honey and gold, set above prominent cheekbones—off his prey.

As he passed the spear he plucked it from the ground and continued to pursue the rabbit. The spear—in Zululand it was called an *assegai*—was a weapon as formidable as it was accurate. But this shorter version, invented by the great Zulu chief, Shaka, was primarily meant for stabbing. Indeed, Shaka himself had always called it an *iklwa*, after the sucking sound the long, broad blade made when withdrawn from its target.

The rabbit darted up a gentle incline and into some bushes. Sam followed it. Here there were obstacles everywhere—prickly pear, many-limbed shin oaks and rocks of varying sizes. But the Zulu weaved his way effortlessly through them, avoiding anything that could slow or injure him, revealing yet another quality—an agility that was nothing less than astonishing.

He sprinted for a few more yards through the tangled brush and then stabbed down with the *assegai,* skewering his prey.

In a second, it was finished.

Standing there under the hard Texas sun, he triumphantly raised the *assegai* and admired the dead cottontail. His startlingly white teeth showed in a triumphant smile, because he knew that neither he nor the man called Jonah would go hungry this night.

Then a new sound caught his attention and abruptly his smile was replaced by a frown. All at once the air was filled with a sound like thunder that wasn't thunder at all; a sound that stirred good memories in him and made the ground beneath his bare feet tremble.

Tireless, he started running back the way he'd come and shortly burst back out onto the riverbank. There he ducked behind a patch of salt-cedar just as a herd of wild mustangs exploded over the crest of a low hill that was a short distance beyond the opposite bank.

Wreathed in sunlit yellow dust, the lead horse was a big, raw-boned, mean-looking albino stallion. He splashed into the center of the river, ears and tail twitching, pink eyes seemingly everywhere at once. Sam judged that he stood sixteen hands at the shoulder, and was of perfect proportions—a strong arched neck, powerful shoulders, a firm back that rose slightly to loins and croup, well-muscled thighs, belly gently curved but in no way heavy or swollen.

The albino turned its head, surveying the area like an emperor surveying his kingdom. Instinctively Sam hunkered lower and held his breath. On the far bank, the rest of the herd and its offspring waited patiently. Through the screening brush, Sam made a quick tally and decided: *amashumi amathathu*—about thirty of them: mostly mares, perhaps two or three other, younger stallions, the rest a mixture of colts and fillies.

Finally the stallion seemed satisfied and stamped a foreleg down, splashing water everywhere.

It was the sign the rest of the herd had been waiting for; all was clear.

They flowed down into and across the river, as much like water themselves, a sea of bay, buckskin, gray and chestnut.

From his hiding place, Sam watched them admiringly. He had a special love of horses, and it was in their company that he felt most comfortable. He owed them his very existence, and was not likely to forget the debt.

When the last mare was up on the opposite bank, the albino whirled around and raced after them. Soon they were lost to sight and silence settled back over the area.

Sam rose and walked slowly out onto the bank. The horses were most likely heading for the distant mountains, where they would be relatively safe from man. Fleetingly he considered going after them. But then he remembered the one called U-Shee-nah, whom he could never leave, and his companion, Jonah, and their supper.

Their supper.

Impulsively he raised the dead cottontail toward the approaching sunset and loosed off a fierce cry of triumph.

"Ingonyama!"

Ingonyama! replied his echo.

And Sam grinned again.

Yes! he thought. *I am lion!*

L ess than twenty minutes later he topped out on the ridge of a low scrub-covered hill and started down the far side, the rabbit carcass flopping loosely on the blade of the *assegai.*

A trail—little more than a thin, wheel-rutted line worn through an otherwise unbroken sea of mesquite—sliced through the broad valley below. At the point where it met the horizon he spied a cloud of dust, backlit by the now-westering sun. Riders, he thought … perhaps a wagon.

By the time he reached the flats, the washed-out, bottle green color of the vehicle had identified it as a stagecoach. Pausing, Sam watched the six-horse team leaning forward into their leathers, each pair—the small wiry leaders, the larger swing animals and finally the heavy-set wheelers—working in perfect harmony with its stable mates. Their clean lines, glistening coats, the flawless movement of muscles made for running, held him entranced, as it always did.

In good humor, he too broke into a run, this time taking a course that would intersect that of the oncoming coach. He vaulted over low bushes, his outstretched legs reaching high to his deep chest as he did so. He weaved between large rocks, never once breaking stride or breathing hard, and within him there burned an exhilaration that only ever came when the wind was in his face and the ground was a blur beneath his feet.

Up on the high rocking seat of the oncoming coach, the grizzled driver jabbed an elbow into his dozing companion's side. The shotgun guard woke with a splutter that left a glisten of spit on his thick black beard. "H-Huh? What—?"

"What the hell's that?" demanded the driver, pointing at something that was moving out on the scrubby plain.

The guard yawned sleepily and squinted off into the distance. "Dunno," he said after a moment. "Looks like a… *man.*"

"A man … " repeated the driver, as if he didn't believe his eyes, " … or an *Injun?*"

The word sent a ripple of fear down each man's spine, for the region had already endured a long, bloody history with the Comanches and their allies, the Kiowas, and it showed no sign of ending any time soon.

"He sure don't *look* like an Injun," said the guard, but he tightened his grip on his ten-gauge coach gun anyway. "'Fact, he don't look much like anythin' I ever *seen* before."

"Well, like it or not, he's headed this way."

"Maybe he needs help."

"He sure don't *look* like he needs help. Look at how *fast* he's comin'!"

The guard had already noticed that; that and the fact that unless the half-naked runner eased up soon, he was going to hit the team broadside on.

The driver gestured toward the coach gun. "Send one o' them there blue whistlers over his head. That ought to discourage him."

"Discourage him from *what,* exactly, Tom? Tryin' to hold us up with nothin' more dangerous than a dead rabbit on a spear?"

The driver glanced about uneasily. "He's the only one we can *see,"* he explained testily. "Who's to say a bunch of red devil buddies ain't hidin' in the nearby brush? We stop for him an' they'll be all over us."

"So don't stop," said the guard.

By now Sam was no more than twenty yards from them, still proudly holding the dead rabbit aloft on his *assegai.* And far from slowing down, he actually sped up and changed course so that he could run alongside the lead horses.

"Naw ... " muttered the driver. "Ain't possible."

"What ain't?"

"Nothin'."

"Go on."

The driver shook his head. "Well, if I didn't know better, I'd say the sonofabitch wants to *race* us."

The guard had never heard anything so crazy, but there was no denying that that was exactly what it looked like. "You know somethin'? I think you might be *right."*

The driver grinned, revealing brown and broken teeth. "Then let's oblige 'im."

He jerked the buckskin-lashed whip from its socket and sent it cracking over the heads of the team. Obediently the horses picked up the pace. The coach lurched unpleasantly and then began to rattle and sway with increased speed.

Sam glanced over his shoulder, smiled at the driver and guard, and also started running faster.

"I'll be damned ... " the guard said admiringly. "Look at that sonuvabuck go!"

But a competitive man by nature, the driver took the challenge personally. He cracked the whip again, sending a gunshot-echo across the plain, and though reluctant to do so, the horses dug deeper, the coach went faster, and Sam dropped back a little, until he was running alongside the swing team.

The trail straightened out and the six-up hitch continued to out-run Sam. The driver grinned and muttered: "That'll learn 'im!" But the grin soured as he realized that Sam was slowly, steadily picking up lost ground again. His pace increased until he was once again running alongside the leaders.

The guard couldn't help it; he cradled the ten-gauge in the crook of one elbow and clapped his delight, cackling: "Well, kiss my ass an' bark like a fox!"

Tom thrust the whip back in its socket, dug a handful of pebbles from his pocket and hurled them at the horses. The stones bounced off their backs like rock-salt buckshot.

Stung, the horses started running even faster. Sam fell back again, past the swing team until it was all he could do to keep parallel with the wheelers.

The coach lurched wildly, tossing its three passengers around. One of them, a middle-aged, sour-faced man with a thin mustache who earlier had introduced himself and his wife as Mr. and Mrs. Thomas Peck of Hobbs,

New Mexico, removed his derby and angrily poked his head out the window.

"You, there! Driver! What in tarnation do you think you're doing?"

Then he saw Sam running alongside the team and became horrified.

"My God—*Indians!*"

The coach bounced over a large rut in the trail and Peck was thrown back inside, where he sprawled across his startled wife's lap. He sat up quickly and started fumbling in his jacket for the .31-caliber Wells Fargo pocket pistol he always carried when traveling. Meanwhile, the third passenger, a tall man in his late twenties, whose well-tailored Norfolk jacket and matching pants concealed a wiry, athletic build, stuck his own head out the window.

Up ahead, the trail began to rise toward a distant, saguaro-studded ridge, and the speed of the coach slowed noticeably as the weary team fought the upgrade. That gave Sam the chance he'd been waiting for. He dug deeper, his legs almost a blur now, and stubbornly began to close in on the lead horses.

The tall man couldn't help but admire his athleticism. Then Peck shoved him aside, pistol in hand.

"What the blazes do you think you're doing?" the tall man demanded, his accent unmistakably British.

"It's all right, Mr. Harris," assured Peck. "One shot from *this* will calm his heathen ways!"

"No!" exclaimed Simon Harris, grabbing for the weapon.

Peck struggled with him. "What do you mean, *no?* We're under attack, sir! By Indians!" Jerking himself free, he poked his head and shoulders out the window, took aim and fired the pistol.

On hearing the shot Sam instantly broke stride and dived into the brush beside the trail. The coach raced on past him. He glared after it and then jumped up as a rooster tail of dust swirled around him.

Ahead, the coach reached the top of the hill and disappeared over the far side ... and once more Zulu Sam felt like the outsider he was.

Inside the coach, Peck was furious. "How *dare* you manhandle me, sir!" he raged at the young Englishman. "Did you *want* that savage horde to lift our scalps?"

His wife gasped at such a dreadful prospect.

Harris eyed him sternly. He had a narrow, freckled face and neatly trimmed, center-parted red hair. Under blond, almost white lashes, his eyes were pale blue. His nose was long and straight and below a handlebar mustache his thin-lipped mouth was faintly contemptuous.

"In the first place," he said, "there was only one man out there, not a savage horde. In the second, he wasn't an Indian, he was a Zulu."

"A *Zulu!* Out here? That's ridiculous!"

"But true, nevertheless," Harris said somewhat pompously. "I spent some time in Africa, sir, in the service of Her Majesty, Queen Victoria, and came into contact with them on a regular basis. Hence, I'd recognize them anywhere. Marvelous specimens! Incredible runners, too! They can run all day and all night ... and still fight a battle when they reach their destination."

"You were a ... military man, Mr. Harris?" asked Peck's wife, calmer now that the Indian scare was over.

"That's correct, madam. I was on the staff of the lieutenant-governor of Natal," he added, deciding that there was no need to tell them that he'd been a mere subaltern—a glorified filing clerk at best.

"How exciting," said Mrs. Peck. "But how did a soldier in the British Army end up here, may I ask?"

"The end of my time in uniform coincided with a bereavement and a small inheritance," Harris replied. He paused, remembering that part of the money had allowed him to buy himself out of the service, which he had come to detest, then added: "Since I was looking for something new to occupy me, my stockbroker suggested I come to the Colonies and invest money in cattle. It's the coming thing, he assures me. And so here I am, looking to purchase land and stock and set myself up as a rancher."

"You'll find it tough," warned Peck. "Tougher than the Africa veldt, I'll warrant, and much tougher indeed than Great Britain."

"But that is precisely what I want, Mr. Peck—a *challenge.* Granted, I will have help, for I've been given an introduction to a certain Major Lawrence Devlin. You've perhaps heard of him?"

"Most definitely," replied Peck. "So has everyone else in New Mexico. His Bar-D Ranch is the biggest in this part of the country. No one knows the cattle business better."

Harris beamed. "I'm to meet the Major at Fort Stockton, where he has promised to show me some good land and supply seed stock at a most advantageous price."

"Excellent," said Peck. "Well, my wife and I wish you nothing but luck, sir." He settled back on the seat. He could have said more, but aware of Major Devlin's ruthless reputation, decided not to. At the same time he couldn't help thinking: *I suspect you'll need it, young man.*

Chapter Two

As Sam jogged tirelessly toward Cathedral Rock, his spirits rose again. Ever since he'd first seen the place, its mysticism had affected him deeply. Everywhere he looked, jagged sandstone bluffs and escarpments clawed skyward, seeming to glow as red as blood in the setting sun. Here an errant evening breeze made a stand of ponderosa pine whisper mysteriously; there a mallard took flight with a mighty flapping of wings, startled by the unexpected appearance of a bass breaking the surface of a stream for air. It was a special place, an ancient place, and one with which Sam felt wholly as one.

He followed a barely discernible trail through canyons and low brush until he came to the camp he and Jonah had set up the day before. Though still some distance out, he paused and deliberately lingered in the lengthening shadows for a time, just to watch his companion.

An eyesore of a wagon stood to one side of a small clearing, its shafts pointed toward the North Star. Many years ago it had been an ambulance. Jonah had bought it from the army before they'd scrapped it altogether, and then painted its sides bright yellow, so that the legend—lettered in a garish bright red— would stand out boldly. The legend read:

DR. Q.M. JONAH
DISCOVERER OF ZULU JUICE
WORLD-FAMOUS ELIXIR AND PANACEA
FOR ACHES, PAINS AND ALL MYSTERIOUS AILMENTS
KNOWN TO MAN
PLUS
MANY YET TO BE DISCOVERED

A tall, spare man of about sixty was peering into the contents of a black cauldron that he'd suspended above a small, rock-ringed fire a short distance from the wagon. His feet were all but hidden by the pile of empty bottles around them. This was Dr. Quincy Martin Jonah, conman extraordinaire.

Jonah was a picture of what used to be and what now was. Once passably handsome, his whiskery face was now jowly and showed the ravaging effects of alcoholism. His watery blue eyes sat in loose pouches. His ears stood proud like open doors. Where once his hair was thick and brown, it had now thinned and lightened to the color of pewter. His battered, dusty high silk hat spoke of a time when he'd had money, and the cut of his rusty black suit had once been all the rage—but not anytime recently. Now it was tight around the shoulders and backside and short in the sleeves, and it was no longer possible for Jonah to button the jacket comfortably. He wore no shirt beneath it, just a stained red undershirt which, like the man himself, had seen better days.

For all that, Jonah was gregarious and jovial by nature, a born thespian with a passion for literature, who had never quite managed to lose his optimism, no matter how much life continued to knock him down.

Presently he was dividing his time between cooking up a fresh batch of 'Zulu juice' in the pot hanging over the fire, and checking a dog-eared recipe to make sure he hadn't left out any of the ingredients.

" … half a cup of molasses … " he muttered, his voice a rich baritone that seemed to relish every word, "nine bottles of whiskey … three gallons of fresh creek water … one tablespoon of mustard … two of asafetida … a plug of chawin' tobacco … uh, of *course!"*

He stuffed the recipe away and patted his pockets until he found the items he sought and had so nearly forgotten to add—

six shriveled green chili peppers. One by one he plopped the peppers into the brew. "Adds flavor," he chuckled, "and keeps the bowels active!"

He seemed to derive unholy pleasure from the word *bowels.*

His work done, Jonah cast a furtive look around to make sure he was alone, then picked up one of the almost-empty whiskey bottles and raised it to his lips. Greedily he drained what little remained. Then, dropping the bottle back onto the pile, he picked up a spindly green stem and poked it into the pot, where he used it to stir the noxious contents.

"Stir well with one creosote branch," he said, "an' let simmer for—"

One of the three horses picketed in a crude rope corral behind him suddenly whinnied. Startled, Jonah looked over his shoulder, the bottles clinking around his ankles. Two of the horses were big and muscular—the team that had hauled them all the way from Wyoming to New Mexico, and on to this Pecos region of southwest Texas. The third was a dainty grullo mare. She was a beautiful slate-gray, with a long black mane, four black stockings, a black stripe down her back and a tiny white star on her pretty, sensitive face.

The mare whinnied again.

"Hush, now," Jonah said softly. "The Chief'll be back soon, I promise. In the meantime, have patience, little lady." And then, raising his voice: "'How poor are they that have not patience! What wound did ever heal but by degrees?' That's Shakespeare, you know."

He turned back to the pot, the movement again making the bottles around his feet clink. He bent, rummaged until he found another one that still contained a few drops of whiskey and was just about to drink from it when he heard Sam approaching. Guiltily he dropped the bottle onto the pile and continued stirring the brew with his creosote branch, whistling casually in an attempt to appear nonchalant.

He made a passable pretence at surprise when Sam finally came into the firelight, but the Zulu wasn't fooled. He glanced meaningfully at the bottles on the ground and then directly into Jonah's face.

Drawing himself up—albeit unsteadily—Jonah said: "What're you giving me *that* look for?"

Sam cocked one eyebrow accusingly.

"I haven't touched a drop!" protested Jonah. "As Voltaire would have it, 'Use, do not abuse; neither abstinence nor excess ever renders man happy.'"

Sam didn't say anything. There wasn't any point. This was a ritual they'd enacted many times before. Instead, the big Zulu thrust the dead cottontail at Jonah, giving the older man no option but to take it. Jonah examined the carcass with clear distaste, but nevertheless settled down to skin it as Sam strode to the horses.

The mare came to him eagerly. He took her head in his hands and fondled her gently. "U-Shee-nah," he murmured, for that was her name.

The mare snuffled softly, as if in answer.

Jonah watched them, struck yet again by the curious bond that tied them. It went deeper than anything he had ever seen before, more than mere affection. There was love between these two. Though Jonah had never experienced it himself, he recognized it when he saw it, and now, as always, he shook his head and concluded philosophically: *Ah, well. Perhaps Governor Wallace was right when he wrote that lonely people will stoop to any companionship.*

After supper Jonah set his tin plate aside and poured himself a mug of coffee. "Want some, Chief?"

It was another ritual between them. He knew that Sam didn't drink coffee. But he always asked just to break the silence between them, for Sam was a man who chose words carefully and spoke them rarely.

Sam shook his head and swallowed his last mouthful of rabbit. He rose from a crouch, wiped his hands on his bare thighs and headed for the wagon, where he drank from the water-barrel dipper.

Jonah watched him, scowling.

"'No thanks, Doc,'" he said with forced joviality, "'I don't care for any right now, but it was right friendly of you to ask. *Right* friendly.'" And then: "'Oh, that's okay, Chief. Hell, what're friends for, if not to keep one another company?'"

But Jonah's sarcasm masked another purpose, for the minute Sam's back was turned he fished out a hip flask and quickly laced his coffee. He only just managed to stuff the flask back out of sight before Sam returned to the fire.

Not sure if he'd been seen, and uneasy because of it, Jonah said more affably: "Sure you, ah, don't want any coffee, Chief?"

Sam only gave him a withering stare.

Faking innocence, Jonah said: *"Now* what?"

By way of answer, Sam snatched up his *assegai* and stabbed it at the older man's chest. The tip of the broad blade connected with the flask inside his jacket with a metallic clink.

"No good," said Sam, his voice a deep rumble.

Jonah shrank back from the spear. "Maybe so. But the trouble, my friend, is that you don't feel the cold like I do. I've got old bones, in case it's escaped your attention! That's the only reason I ever touch the stuff. And that's the God's honest truth."

Sam grunted his displeasure, took a small whetstone from his buckskin breechclout and began to sharpen the blade of the *assegai* on it.

Jonah watched him for a while. Then, to relieve the heavy silence he said: "Better quit doing that, Chief. If you're not careful you'll wear that blade down to nothing."

Sam ignored him.

"What'll you do *then*, uh?" Jonah added. "When you don't have that fancy spear to hunt with?"

Sam ran the edge of the blade gently across his palm to test its sharpness. A thin ribbon of blood appeared, making Jonah feel decidedly queasy.

"By then," Sam said grimly, "I will be back with my own people."

"Well, I sure *hope* so," said Jonah. But try as he might, he was unable to summon any real conviction to back up the words. "'Course, passage on one of those fancy ships costs plenty. But if business gets better, and you win the big race tomorrow … well, in no time a-tall you'll be on your way back to Africa."

Neither of them really believed that. But to acknowledge the fact that he would never see his homeland again was something Zulu Sam wasn't sure even he could handle.

Moodily he rose and walked back over to the rope corral. As he untied the knotted lariat and led the grullo out of the makeshift pen, Jonah called: "What the—? Where you reckon *you're* going?"

"To run with U-Shee-nah."

"Oh-h-h no!" said Jonah, climbing clumsily to his feet. "You're not going *anywhere* the night before a big race, and that's—"

Sam merely led the mare past him.

"All right—go ahead!" Jonah called after him. "You never listen to me, anyway! But I'm warning you, Chief. You tire yourself out tonight, and tomorrow every damn cripple in *town'll* be able to beat you!"

Sam stopped and regarded him with eyes that were unreadable. The 'big race' was one of the things that had brought them to the Pecos to begin with. It was being held at Fort Stockton as part of the garrison town's carnival week. In addition to the annual foot race there would be wrestling, horse-racing, a turkey-shoot and a pie-eating contest. Sam would have been happy to avoid the entire thing, but carnival weeks were good for Jonah's trade and they could always use the extra money Sam could make from winning races.

At last the big Zulu said: "Sam can run all night—for many nights—and still beat everyone tomorrow."

He then set off into the desert beyond the canyon, the mare following him like an obedient puppy.

Jonah watched them go. After a while he picked up a medicine bottle and a funnel, and began preparing his stock for tomorrow.

Chapter Three

Sam and U-Shee-nah ran side by side across the moon-washed flats until they reached a high point that overlooked the broken country below. While the mare wandered off to explore their surroundings, Sam dropped to one knee and studied the velvet bowl of star-speckled sky above. There was a strange peacefulness in the heavens. Sam felt comforted by it—until he thought of his home and how unlikely it was that he'd ever see it again.

Much as he wanted to, he knew better than to beseech his god, Umvelinquangi, for help. Umvelinquangi was too high, too holy and too pure to be approached. But he *did* reach out and ask his ancestral spirit, Amatongo, to aid him. After all, he had come this far by his own efforts. Could he not now expect some help to return to his own people?

He'd been wrenched from his homeland three years earlier, one of only a handful of Zulus ever to be taken for the slave trade. That alone was shame enough. The Zulu was master of his domain, each man a fierce warrior that other tribes knew best to leave alone. But one day he and a small group of friends had gone off in pursuit of a leopard that had been terrorizing their village. They were young, and though the hunt was dangerous it promised excitement and a chance to prove one's courage.

As it turned out, the leopard's tracks had led them far from home, and that night they had camped on scrub-covered veldt with the intention of returning to their village the following day.

They weren't worried. This wasn't the first time they had slept outside the village. But this time, just before dawn, they had been surprised by a gang of Portuguese slavers armed with what Sam then called fire-sticks and now knew to be guns. The Portuguese had said they were bad spirits, and that Sam and his friends would be killed unless they did as they were told. The deception scared Sam's friends, but not Sam himself. He had no doubt that these were just men—albeit evil ones. And so he awaited his chance to escape, and in whispers advised his brothers to do likewise.

Unfortunately, the chance never came.

Taken captive, he and his companions were marched sixty miles east, and flogged regularly for even the slightest transgression. Eventually they came to the coast, and the awe-inspiring sight of the great Indian Ocean. Here a stinking nightmare of a three-master rode at anchor, its crew eagerly awaiting its fresh cargo of slaves.

Clapped in irons, Sam and his friends were thrown into a dark hold below decks. Here he could only listen to the sobbing of prisoners from other tribes as well as his own, who by now felt that they had somehow angered Unkulunkulu, the Mightiest of the Mighty, and that this was his way of punishing them. Their sobbing, together with the shrieks of the women and children who had been stolen away from their villages by other slavers, combined to make a sound of despair that almost drove him mad.

To fight it, he grew even more determined to escape. He loved his homeland. It was all he had ever known, and he would not be taken from it. But then the ship set sail, and the sea threw it up and down as if it was but a toy in the hands of a vindictive child, and soon he became too ill to think about anything but his own suffering.

Eventually the malaise and poor diet, the cramped conditions and the lack of good, clean air, took its toll. Like so many of his friends, he soon fell into a kind of daze, not always entirely aware of the change from one day to the next.

Sometimes they were allowed up on deck, there to feel sick at the vastness of the ocean as hungry gannets shrieked overhead. Oft-times the water boiled with fish the Portuguese called *sardinha:* and often, too, scores of copper sharks would herd the sardines into a packed mass and then there would be a feeding frenzy, and the wake would turn from white to red.

Even if one could still hope by now to swim back to shore in his leg irons, then, the sharks would catch him long before that distant shore ever drew into sight.

It was a salutary lesson.

But long weeks later, land *did* show on the horizon. Sam heard the crew call it *'América.'* Later, he learned that the place where he and his companions were taken ashore under cover of darkness was called the State of Alabama. He learned also that the Portuguese had been employed by a businessman who grew cotton in a fertile basin called the Tennessee Valley, and wanted cheap labor to pick it.

Beaten down and overawed by his new surroundings, Sam picked cotton and took brutal, unwarranted beatings for the next eight months. During that time he heard much talk about other places in this *América,* where men were not held as slaves; places with names like Pennsylvania and Massachusetts, Indiana, Iowa, Michigan and the Territory of Kansas. It was said that many runaway slaves had headed for these northern regions before him, while others had escaped to a different country altogether—a place called Canada.

But many more had been dragged back in chains and punished severely.

A slave was an investment; his owner spared little effort in bringing him back. Bounties were posted and white men whose trade it was hunted them down with any means at their disposal. And when they were returned to their owners they were whipped, or branded, or suffered amputation of limbs, as an example to others.

Perhaps it was true, then, what his friend Dingane, had said one humid afternoon: *"AkiCmmango umgena'liba."*
In this land there is no hillside without a grave.

But Sam decided that they would have to catch him before they could punish him … and he had no intention of allowing himself to be caught.

He thought about it for many nights and told no one of his plans lest a careless slip betray him. But it seemed to him that he should stand the best chance of all if he were to go in the one direction no one would ever suspect—west. He had no idea what lay in that vast section of the country, but he had heard stories of the land and the freedom to be had there.

And so he set his sights on escape, and when a tropical storm rolled in from the Gulf one night, he finally made his move.

No one with any sense would have dared to escape in such conditions, so no one was expecting it. Sneaking away into the night, he was quickly drenched to the skin. Teeth chattering—for the usually oppressive temperature had plummeted—he splashed and slid through a morass of mud that oozed up around his ankles, seeking the relative safely of a stand of pecans that bordered one of the fields.

The elements fought him every step of the way. Thunder boomed overhead. Lightning showed him brief, pale images of his gale-blown surroundings. Torrential rain slashed his face and wind buffeted him from his course. Even his seemingly boundless energy was quickly sapped. But his will remained as strong as ever.

He plunged on through the darkness, determined to put as much distance between him and the plantation as possible. The rain, he told himself, was a good, cleansing thing. They could set hounds on his trail, but they would find nothing of his scent. Even his footprints would be washed away.

As it turned out, there was no pursuit—at least none he was ever aware of. But at no time did he dare relax his guard. When he used roads at all, he tried to stick to seldom-used ones. And always he tried to move under cover of darkness, holing up wherever he could by day. It was during these times that he fashioned his first crude spear, promising himself that one day he would replace it with the weapon of his people, the *assegai*.

When he could, he hunted for game. When game was sparse, he stole what he needed to survive. And always, he followed the setting sun to the west ... to the west, and a new life.

Of course, he had no idea how big this *América* was. Perhaps if he had, he never would have set out on his journey. Mile followed mile, became ten, a hundred, eventually a thousand. And every yard of the way he felt like a hunted animal, sleeping light and for little more than an hour at a stretch, often going without food. He avoided everyone, so that none would ever know of his passing. His new life pared him down to muscle and bone; it blistered his feet, cramped his muscles ... and much as he hated to admit it, even to himself, it began to wear away his spirit.

The elements did the rest. Scalding days followed by freezing nights, rain and sometimes snow—which was an entirely new experience for him—and cruel, buffeting winds.

Loneliness, hopelessness, a gradual conviction that he would die long before he found the freedom that meant so much to him ...

How far did he still have to go, anyway, before he reached this place he had heard about, where a man could live free? Where was he *now?* The desert in which he found himself gave him no clues.

It had been noon of a harsh day, he remembered, and his blistered ebony skin was peeling. His dry lips were cracked, his sandpaper tongue swollen. He had told himself to march on, that somewhere up ahead there would be water, and water would give back the strength he had lost and now needed so badly.

But finally his legs buckled under him. He collapsed, face-down in the hot sand, knowing that he could go no farther.

There would be no moving on from this place: this was where he would die.

As life ebbed out of him, his final, shallow breaths made the tiny, golden grains of sand skitter and dance around his mouth and nostrils. The world grew dark and silent … dark and silent … and he felt himself drifting away and was too exhausted to even *try* to fight it …

And then he'd heard it.

The sound made him stir and come back from whatever final journey upon which he had been about to embark. He pushed himself up on his knees and gazed weakly at the endless flats of the desert surrounding him. His eyes narrowed against the glare, their whites shot through with blood.

The mare stood about two hundred yards to the east, looking at him. She was small, wiry and tight-muscled, with a glossy coat as brown as the Zulu's own blistered skin.

He looked back at the horse. It was the first sign of life he had seen since … he couldn't remember when. But the mare looked strong, not at all as gaunt and worn down as he was. Which meant …

Which meant there had to be food and water around here somewhere.

To this day he still didn't know where he found the strength to stand up, but he did. He stood and began to shuffle toward the horse. The mare watched him approach for a while, then tossed its head, turned and began to trot away.

"Cha!" he cried. *"Cha! Ngilahlekile!"*

The mare paid no attention, in essence giving him no choice but to follow her.

Somehow he found it within him to jog after the horse. A half-mile later the mare joined a dozen other horses around a small, shallow basin filled with water.

At first Sam thought his eyes were deceiving him. It couldn't be …

Then he threw himself into the water. Grateful for the chill it sent through him, he came up gasping for air. Then he sat there, up to his waist, happily splashing himself and gulping down big mouthfuls of water that cooled his parched throat. It was only water, but nothing had ever tasted so sweet.

Within moments his shriveled stomach threw up the water and he thought he was going to die again. Then his head cleared, he drank some more and this time kept it down.

The other horses watched his every move curiously, but with no fear. Not seeing him as a threat, the stallion whose herd this was simply ignored him. He had a harem of mares, but one that looked older than the rest seemed to be his favorite.

After a while Sam—though he was not called that then—crawled out of the basin and flopped down on the sand. The water had revived him, but he knew he wasn't out of the woods yet. His stomach growled, reminding him how long it had been since he'd last eaten.

He sat up. His vision was sharper now, as was his thinking. But the desert looked as empty and devoid of life as ever.

The mare that had saved his life nickered softly and Sam glanced at her. Behind her, a few of the other horses had wandered off to graze on some nearby scrub-grass.

Sam watched as they methodically chewed away, listened to the soft tearing sounds they made tugging the shoots free ... and then he laughed. He laughed and continued laughing until his sides ached, because the horses were telling him something he himself had been too dumb to realize—that there was food everywhere out here, if only a man knew where to find it ... just as their was in his own homeland.

He drank again and began a cautious search. By trial and error he discovered that the fruit of the prickly pear was good. The fruit of the saguaro was a sweet red pulp littered with crisp seeds. The beans of the mesquite were also filling. But when he found the likes of locoweed and nightshade, instinct told him to avoid them. Unlike so many other plants, these were shunned by packrats and Gila monsters.

From that day forward Sam's education began in earnest. As was his custom, he ate well but sparingly. He learned that water was most likely to be found at the base of hills, and that occasionally he could find it by noting the direction in which birds flew. He learned to avoid plants that yielded a milky white sap when cut, and to eat only berries that wild animals ate.

He also learned about horses, and was still doing so, even now. He learned that he could tell how they were feeling by reading their facial expressions. Ears, eyes, the flaring of their nostrils—everything meant something. And when they flattened their ears or cow-kicked, he knew to keep away from them.

He soon learned that horses possessed intelligence and spirit, and over time realized that the stallion stole mares from other herds. It fought off the bachelor herds when they came seeking mates; yet strangely, whenever the stallion and its mares were around Sam, they became surprisingly obedient.

As the months went by and his fitness returned, he learned to run with them, to become as one with them.

It was then he had fallen in with Jonah, who christened him Zulu Sam because he was unable to pronounce Sam's real name. Sam pretended to have no patience with Jonah, but in a strange way he reminded the Zulu of his father, and slowly he began to develop an affection for him.

For better or worse, they were together now, these two curious companions. And if it was true, and Sam really *was* destined never to see his beloved homeland again, then he could think of no better man to share his new life with … though he would sooner die than ever let Jonah know as much.

Chapter Four

Fort Stockton had started life as a small U.S. Army post built beside a natural waterhole known as Comanche Springs. Now, a decade later, a sizeable town had grown up around the adobe-walled garrison and its annex, which lay half a mile northeast.

Celebrations were well underway by the time Jonah drove his wagon onto busy Main Street. The local brass band was playing a lively rendition of *Annie Lisle,* while banners stretching from one side of the street to the other announced:

> *FORT STOCKTON CARNIVAL WEEK!*
> *WELCOME ALL CONTESTANTS!*
> *FREE DRINKS AT THE CRYSTAL PALACE FOR ALL*
> *WINNERS!*

As near as he could tell, the town seemed to be a typical mixture of Americans and Mexicans, with Americans forming the majority. Jonah identified visiting ranchers and businessmen among the half-breeds, women, children, the black on- and off-duty soldiers and tame Indians. But if accents were anything to go by, he reckoned Fort Stockton also had more than its share of Europeans and Irishmen, too. It was, then, a regular metropolis ... which meant that business should be good.

Carnival booths had been erected everywhere, sharply attired barkers doing their best to draw the attention of the crowds. Here townsmen were using crossbows to hit targets and win prizes; there a group of cowboys were competing in a fast-draw contest, with the owner of the booth timing each contestant in turn with an old railroad timepiece. Farther along the street they passed a gingham-covered trestle table that sagged beneath a mountain of pies. Onlookers were cheering the chubby contestants on as each sought to eat as many pies as he could and be declared the winner.

As always, their entrance created a stir. These people had all seen traveling medicine shows before, of course ... but they'd never seen anything like Sam, especially the way he looked right then, as he walked proudly ahead of the team down the center of the street.

He wore a single white ostrich plume at the front of his head-ring, two white-feather armlets and more feathers attached below his knees. He carried an oval Zulu war-shield in one hand and his *assegai* in the other.

"Howdy, folks!" called Jonah, doffing his hat to right and left. "You, there, you boys! Stand well back, if you please! The Chief here don't like to be crowded—and that spear he's holding, well, that's just about sharper than your father's razor!"

The boys Jonah had addressed stared awestruck at Sam and he walked past them. The remark also had the desired effect on the crowd, as Jonah had known it would. Everyone seemed to shrink back and yet crane forward at the same time, to get a better look at this tall, muscular warrior who reminded them of the buffalo soldiers garrisoned at Fort Stockton and yet was so very different.

"Come on, folks, don't get left behind!" Jonah continued. "Inside this here wagon are the last remaining bottles of a medicinal cure-all that guarantees to fix what ails you and shave years off your age! Its name is so sacred that only witchdoctors dare speak it, and even then only in a whisper. That's why I call it Zulu juice, because I promised those wise old men I met in Central Africa all those years ago that I'd never share its rightful name with another living soul!

"So come one, come all, each man and his mate! For it's you lucky people who'll get the chance to buy the last few bottles of this wondrous elixir, this ambrosia not of the gods but of anyone willing to invest one dollar—that's right, folks, you heard me, just *one* lousy dollar—in their health and longevity!"

A vacant lot stood between Fountain's Funeral Parlor and Nelson's Feed and Grain. Jonah called, *"Chief!"* and Sam led them onto it. There, Jonah climbed down and walked around to the back of the wagon, which was now facing the growing crowd. Sam followed him, unhitching U-Shee-nah from the doorknob there and tethering her to a wheel instead. He then stood, sentry-like, beside the open doors with his arms folded and face impassive, just the way Jonah had taught him.

The ambulance was stacked high with bottle-filled cartons. Jonah grabbed the nearest bottle by its neck and held it up for the crowd to inspect. All they could see was that it contained a murky brown liquid.

"Come on, folks, don't be shy! Step a little closer and take a look at the one thing in this world that can guarantee you a long and healthy life! I'm sure intelligent folks like yourselves have read about it at one time or another, in the scientific papers, that is. No white man has ever fully understood its properties, except yours truly, of course! And it's for sure that no white man will ever manage to replicate the subtle and—yes, I'll confess it, *surprising*—blend of herbs, spices and secret ingredients known only to the great Zulu tribe of Africa … and of course, my humble self.

"But alas! Even *I* can no longer brew this grand elixir, for I lost the recipe in a river crossing not two months ago! And that is why what you see here, ladies and gentlemen, is the last remaining batch of Zulu juice! Once it's gone, it's gone! There will be no more … unless some other brave soul risks life and limb to return to the Dark Continent and attempt to win the trust of the Zulu people, as did I!"

Jonah uncorked the bottle and raised it to his lips. The crowd watched with gaping mouths. He took a healthy pull, wiped the neck on his sleeve and shoved the cork back with the heel of his hand.

"Yes …. yes … " he muttered, and gave a theatrical shiver. "I can feel it moving through my body, energizing me after my long journey, bringing strength back to my tired muscles. And as for my mental faculties … ? My goodness, ladies and gentlemen, I can remember practically every day of my life with crystal clarity, remember the sum knowledge of everything I have learned and which, without the benefit of Zulu juice, age would have made me forget!"

"What about the recipe you lost?" called someone from the back of the crowd. "Can't it make you remember *that?*"

Jonah's lips thinned. "Would that it could!" he replied with a flourish. "But let me ask you something, young man! What choice would *you* make, between a recipe that was written down before you, and one that you could only *recall?* The balance of these ingredients is so sensitive that to err in the quantity of even one of them would be to render the juice all but useless!

"Now, I could mix up any so-called 'remedy' and sell it to you, and you'd buy it and try it and then want to cover me in tar and feathers because it did nothing for you at all—and you'd be right to want to do that, for I would be little more than a charlatan! But such is not in my nature, folks. My word is my bond, known to many and broken to none! Besides, honesty was, is and will always remain the best policy in all matters!

"And so I come before you today with the one, the only, the genuine article!"

He studied the crowd shrewdly, enjoying the power of holding them within his thrall.

"And yet I can see doubt in your expressions," he admitted. "Well, my friends, you are *right* to be cynical. I have seen the same phony 'professors' as you! Fly-by-nights, the pack of them, with not a single qualification to their names! But in Dr Quincy Martin Jonah you have before you the real McCoy!"

"Make up your mind, Doc!" called a young man who had pushed his way to the front of the assembly. "Is you called Jonah or McCoy?"

The crowd laughed at the sally. So did Jonah, fortifying himself with another swig from the bottle as he did so. "Right you are, young man! I can take a hint! I've been extolling the virtues of this here Zulu juice for long enough, and you've all grown tired of my voice, as smooth and honeyed as it may be. So—what remains to convince you that I am telling the truth? Why, the evidence of your own *eyes,* that's what!"

A buzz went through the onlookers, and Jonah knew he had snared them again at just the moment when it seemed they might wriggle off his metaphorical hook.

"You see, folks," he said, "I don't have to say another word about this here answer to all of man's ails! And you know *why?* Because my companion, the Chief, here, is all the proof I need to show you good people! Take a look at him! Have you ever seen a finer specimen of manhood? I thought not! But how old do you suppose he is?"

At first no one answered. Then someone off to the left said: "Twenty."

"Twenty-five," called another.

A few nods confirmed that this seemed a reasonable assumption.

Jonah shook his head. "My friends—for so you are—the great chief here has just celebrated his *fiftieth* birthday!"

The word *fifty* rippled through the crowd. The onlookers were by turns awed, surprised or downright suspicious.

"By God, he ain't no fifty!" called one man.

"If'n he's fifty, then my ol' gran'pappy, he must be *six hundred* an' fifty!"

Jonah looked unconcerned. "It's all right, folks. I don't blame you for doubting me. 'Fact is, till I saw for myself what

Zulu Juice can do for a man—a Zulu, like the Chief here, only three times his age … well, I was doubtful myself … "

An elderly woman whose small features were gathered together in the center of her pinched face, called: "What did it do, young man?"

"Do, you say?" replied Jonah, laughing. "Well, ma'am, I'll tell you. It made that tired, wrinkled old Zulu feel *young* again. That's right, folks! You heard me. So young, in fact, that he up and grabbed himself the nearest young gal he could find, and … well, let's just say he started increasing the population of his village with as much vigor as a jackrabbit!"

The crowd laughed again, now well and truly won over by Jonah, and his promise of youth and virility. The elderly woman immediately delved into her tapestry purse.

"Here—I'll take a bottle!"

Jonah snatched up a bottle from his supply and handed it over, taking a dollar bill in return.

As soon as money had changed hands, she uncorked the bottle, took an experimental sniff, then drank a healthy swallow. The silent crowd watched for a reaction, but nothing happened immediately. Finally the old woman smacked her lips and smiled contentedly.

"Feel any younger yet, Missus Farley?" asked another woman in the crowd.

Mrs. Farley pondered the question briefly. "I don't know about feelin' any younger," she replied, "but I sure feel a whole lot more content with my lot!"

"Okay, folks," cried Jonah. "Who's next?"

Hands clutching dollar bills sprang up like weeds. Jonah could hardly sell his wares fast enough. He could have used a little help from Sam, but a quick glance told him that Sam's mind was elsewhere right then, his attention fixed on two cowboys who, bored with Jonah's spiel, had started examining U-Shee-nah with the appreciative eye of men born to the saddle.

Feeling the need to protect the mare, Sam stepped forward, raising his *assegai*. The cowboys, seeing him come, immediately backed off.

"That's it, folks," urged Jonah, still passing out bottles and raking in dollars. "Get 'em while they last!"

Those who had already bought their bottles drifted away to uncork them and sample the contents, and Jonah was suddenly so busy taking money, making change and handing over bottle after bottle that he wasn't immediately aware that an ominous hush began to settle over the crowd.

When he finally realized something was wrong he looked up and saw a big, barrel-chested man elbowing slowly through the spectators towards him. A man with the badge of a town marshal pinned to his shirt.

Thinking fast, he said: "Well, howdy, Marshal! I was *just* coming to see you!"

The marshal greeted that comment with a cold stare and a long, hard silence. He was about six feet even, with a round, pugilist's face and dark, deep-set eyes. He was fifty or thereabouts, with broad shoulders that stretched at the shoulders of his red placket shirt, and a belly that overhung his gunbelt. Even so, there was no doubting the power he still possessed. Here was a man with an iron will, who took no sass from anyone and never had.

Suddenly, moving so fast Jonah didn't even see it coming, the marshal snatched a bottle of Zulu juice from Jonah's hand, tore out the cork, sniffed and grimaced. Very deliberately, he upturned the bottle and emptied its contents into the thirsty dust at his feet.

"Hey!" protested Jonah. "Just hold on a minute, marshal …"

"Name's McCabe," growled the lawman. His voice was like gravel dropping on a coffin lid. "Alexander McCabe."

Jonah backed down. "An old and, ah, revered patronym, Marshal. A Scotsman, eh? I once knew a Scotsman in—"

"What's your name, mister?" asked McCabe.

"Quincy Martin Jonah," Jonah replied proudly. "Doctor of Medicine."

"Got a permit to sell whiskey?"

"*Whiskey?* Why, Marshal, this isn't *whiskey*. It's a patented medicine called—"

"I could lock you up for this, you know."

"But ... but, Marshal, it's no crime to want to *help* folks, is it?"

"These folks don't need your kind of help," grumbled the marshal. "They's plenty enough whiskey on offer in this town as it is." At last he seemed to notice Sam, and his scowl deepened. "What the hell is *that?*" he asked.

"*That*, Marshal, is my friend and colleague, the Chief. A real, live Zulu warrior from darkest Africa!"

"He friendly?"

"The Chief? Oh, sure! Real friendly. Fact is, Zulus are famous for their friendliness—"

"Well, he don't *look* too friendly, way he's holdin' that there spear. Make him drop it."

Sam had been listening to the exchange. Now he raised the *assegai* defiantly, for no Zulu ever surrendered his weapon voluntarily.

McCabe drew his Colt. "Make him drop it, Jonah! Now, 'fore I put a bullet in him."

Realizing the marshal meant it, Jonah quickly put a hand on the arm holding the spear and tried to make Sam lower it. "Take it easy, Chief."

The Zulu resisted, never once taking his eyes from the marshal.

The marshal thumbed back the hammer of his Colt. Around him, the crowd shrank back to avoid the inevitable spray of blood.

"You got another second, mister," growled McCabe.

"Chief—"

"Time's up," McCabe said.

Impulsively Jonah stepped in front of Sam. "No need for that," he said hurriedly. Out of the corner of his mouth he stage-whispered: "Put the goddamn spear down, you idiot!"

At last Sam lowered the weapon.

"There you go, marshal," said Jonah, trying to hide his relief. "No harm done. Just a little misunderstanding on the Chief's part is all, and easy enough to understand. I mean, living in the wilds of Africa all his life, he—"

"That's enough," growled McCabe. He turned to the crowd, adding: "Rest of you, go on about your business! *Go on! Show's over, here. Now—git!*"

Grudgingly the crowd broke up and began to move away.

McCabe watched them sourly. At length he turned back to Jonah and Sam and said sternly: "I'll let it slide this time, Jonah. But I see you peddlin' this joy-juice to anyone again, I'll lock you up faster'n you can blink, the pair of you! Understand?"

"S-Sure, Marshal," Jonah said. "You're a man of uncommon mercy, sir, and I salute you for—"

But McCabe was already striding away.

Jonah sagged and, when he was sure the lawman was out of earshot, muttered, "Marshal, if I was a dog and you were a flower, I'd lift up my leg and give you a shower."

Chapter Five

With no chance of selling any more Zulu juice in Fort Stockton, at least for as long as McCabe was marshal, Jonah decided to park the wagon outside of town and go drum up some favorable odds for that afternoon's foot race. Again Sam led the way, striding imperiously down the center of Main with the old converted ambulance rocking along behind him.

A group of cowboys had gathered beside the public corral next to the stable. Some of them were sitting atop the fence, others leaning against it, all of them enjoying what was happening in the corral itself.

Jonah, hearing the cowboys' whooping and whistling their encouragement, reined up near the corral and saw that they were watching a young woman riding a golden sorrel with a flowing flaxen mane and tail. The horse was a magnificent specimen, but the woman, too, was something to behold.

Jonah guessed she was in her mid-twenties. He also realized she was beautiful—eye-catchingly so. Tall for a woman, she looked attractively lithe and slim in a boy's white shirt and jeans and custom, hand-tooled boots. She had long butter-colored hair that spilled from under a wide-brimmed white Stetson and her skin was smooth and unspoiled by the harsh desert sun. She also rode with uncommon grace.

"A man could ride a long ways before he came across a prettier sight than that," he muttered.

Sam had also noticed horse and rider, and now strode to the fence to get a better look. The cowboys stiffened, not sure what to make of him. Maybe sensing their disquiet, the girl on the sorrel turned, glanced briefly at Sam and then—

—then she saw U-Shee-nah, once again tethered to the doorknob at the back of the old ambulance, her coat gleaming like polished blue silver in the sunlight.

A moment later Jonah snapped the reins, and as the wagon trundled on, called: "Come on, Chief. Let's find some shade and water these horses."

Sam remained where he was for a few seconds more, his amber-gold eyes following the lines of the sorrel, the effortless way in which it did whatever its mistress demanded of it.

When he finally turned and strode off after the ambulance, one of the cowboys, a lean, wiry fellow called Wes Rivers, eyed him critically. He was an odd-looking man. His head looked too big for his body, a big Adam's apple protruded from his skinny neck, and his shaggy black hair hung to his shoulders. "Lon," he drawled, "jes' what do you suppose he is?"

Lon Cory, shorter, with dark good looks, shrugged. "Some kind of Mex' or Injun, I reckon."

But the cowboy next to them, Rafe Hamblin, a stocky man with wiry red hair and a gunfighter's mustache, shook his head. "Uh-uh. That's one of them there African native fellers. A-rabs, they call 'em."

"A-rabs? You're funnin' me, right?"

"Uh-uh." Hamlin grinned, drained the beer he was holding and tossed the bottle. Then drawing his Colt, he said: "Two bits says I can cut off his feather, without him even knowin' it's gone!"

Rivers, who like the others had been drinking since they'd hit town, didn't hesitate. "You're on!" he grinned.

Around him, the rest of the cowboys eagerly turned to watch.

Hamlin stepped out into the street. He wasn't tall but he was strong, with thick arms and a flat belly. Too much beer made him unsteady, but he still managed to extend his gun-arm.

Closing one blue eye, he aimed the Colt toward Sam—and fired.

The gunshot shattered every other sound on Main Street. A split second later the top half of the ostrich plume in Sam's headpiece exploded into the air and then floated down before his face.

The Zulu reacted immediately.

Turning, he dropped to a crouch and threw the *assegai* in one fluid motion.

It flew straight—for once—the point burying itself in the dirt between Rafe Hamblin's feet. Startled, he jumped sideways with yelp. But even as he looked up from the short, quivering spear he saw Sam sprinting back toward him, and prepared to fire again.

Sam leaped gracefully into the air and dropkicked the cowboy. Hamblin staggered back, firing off a wild shot, and went sprawling.

Recovering, he jumped up and swung wildly at Sam's head. The Zulu avoided the blow, grabbed Hamblin around the waist and threw him toward the corral. The cowboys by the fence scattered as Hamblin slammed against a post.

Dazed, he lay there a moment shaking his head. Around him his friends yelled for him to get up and fight.

Sam stood there, chest heaving, awaiting Hamblin's next move.

When Hamblin finally obliged him, it was to grab a Barlow knife from his back pocket. In one savage motion he unpeeled the larger of its two blades from the teardrop-shaped handle and then slowly got up, the knife slicing the air in front of him.

Sam jumped back to avoid the slashing blade, then grabbed Hamblin's wrist and twisted his arm up behind his back. Hamblin yelped and tried to jerk free. But Sam only increased the pressure on Hamlin's arm, forcing to the cowboy to grunt with pain.

"You no move," Sam told him, "or I break arm."

Hamlin had no choice but to obey.

It was then a big, thick-fingered hand clamped on Sam's shoulder.

"Let him go, mister."

Sam stiffened.

"You heard me. Let him go."

Sam released Hamlin's wrist and turned to face the newcomer.

He found himself looking into cool, incisive gray eyes that belonged to a tall, wide-shouldered, flat-bellied man in his early thirties. He was handsome in a rugged, weathered fashion and exuded a quiet honesty that made Sam had not seen often in this land. Dressed in range clothes, he wore a gunbelt buckled around his waist. The Colt that belonged in the holster was now gripped his right hand, the muzzle aimed at Sam's muscular belly.

The two men studied each other, long and hard. Then the newcomer, satisfied that there would be no further trouble, relaxed and holstered his Colt. He then pulled the *assegai* from the dirt, examined it briefly but with no real curiosity, and dropped it at Sam's feet.

"My name's Prince, mister," he said. "Jim Prince, foreman of the Bar D. You try a stunt like that again and I'll make you *swallow* that there pig-sticker."

Jonah jumped down from the ambulance and hurried over. "Now see here! Before you start dispensing your own brand of justice, that fellow there started it!" He thumbed at Hamlin. "He fired a shot at—!"

Prince cut him off. "I saw what he did. And I ain't excusin' it. But Rafe Hamblin rides for the brand, and when you take on one of us, you take on the lot."

Jonah started to argue, then decided that there was nothing to gain by defiance. "'He who commits injustice is ever made more wretched than he who suffers it,'" he quoted. "Plato."

"Fancy talk don't impress anyone around here," Prince said, "—least of all me. So, if I was you, I'd move on 'fore there's any more trouble."

Jonah, knowing when to fold, nudged Sam. "Come on, Chief. The horses need watering."

Sam stared at Prince for another moment and then picked up the *assegai.* Together, he and Jonah walked to the ambulance. There, Jonah climbed onto the seat and grabbed the reins while Sam remained on his feet, every inch a warrior who knew no fear.

It was then the blonde girl rode her sorrel up to the corral fence.

"He's all yours, Jim," she said, dismounting and handing the reins to the foreman.

Prince smiled at her. She was his boss's daughter, Charlotte Devlin, and he was hopelessly in love with her. But he knew that being only a hired hand was a barrier he'd never overcome, so he loved her from a distance, and Charlotte— Charlie, as she preferred to be called—barely even knew he was there.

Besides, Charlie only had eyes for the grullo mare right then.

"Beautiful, isn't she, Jim?"

Prince nodded.

"Wonder if she's for sale?"

"Like the Major says, Miss Charlie—everything's for sale … if you got the money to meet the price. And the Major's sure got that."

Charlie smiled at him. "You're wrong there," she said, rubbing her palm along the sorrel's sleek neck. "Brandy will *never* be for sale."

"Everything but Brandy, then," he said, adding impulsively: "An' o' course *you,* Miss Charlie."

Chapter Six

Later, when Charlie and Prince entered the lobby of the Silver Spur Hotel, they found her father, Major Lawrence Devlin, in conversation with his visitor from England.

When they'd met Simon Harris off the stage the evening before, her father had said something about helping Harris establish himself as a rancher in the region. But Charlie knew her father rarely did anything without an ulterior motive. In this case, she guessed it was more than just the chance to make a quick profit off a gullible foreigner.

As they'd signed him into the Silver Spur, where the Major had a permanent suite, her father had extolled all of Harris's many virtues; that he came from an aristocratic English family, had served his country in Africa, was a fine athlete and wanted to settle in the Pecos region.

She'd guessed at once what her father was up to. If he could somehow encourage her interest in Harris, then it was possible that marriage would eventually follow … and that would satisfy him on two counts. Through marriage her father could eventually add Harris's land to his own and make the Bar D even bigger, and with any luck their union would produce the grandsons he so desired to keep the family bloodline flowing.

That was fine, except for one thing—she, Charlie, wasn't interested in Harris.

As she approached them now, her father turned to her with a beaming smile. "Guess what, Charlie, Simon is going to enter the foot race this afternoon!"

Devlin was a tall man with dark, almost swarthy good looks, who still carried himself like the Confederate officer he had once been. His face was long and slender, with dark

45

brows, graying muttonchops and a clipped black cavalry mustache. Immaculate in a two-piece suit and muley hat, he could be effortlessly charming when it suited him. But when it didn't, he could display a short temper and a ruthless streak that Charlie herself had never quite been able to reconcile.

Harris grinned bashfully. "Well, I don't believe I should crow, but I won more than my share of cups at school, and I've maintained my interest in sport ever since."

"Well, I wish you luck," Charlie said politely.

"Luck doesn't play much of a part, if you take it seriously," Harris assured her. "It's a *science,* Miss Devlin. A matter of style, determination, self-confidence and performance."

"As you say," she said and turned back to her father. "Daddy, I've just seen the prettiest little grullo mare. She'd be just perfect—"

"Now, Charlie, don't exaggerate," her father interrupted in his usual patronizing way. "God made just one perfect horse, and I have the good fortune to own him."

"I wasn't comparing her to Brandy, Daddy. I just said—"

"You want me to buy her for you, is that it?" he said indulgently.

"Will you? Jim saw her, and he agrees—"

"Do you, Jim?"

Prince shrugged. "She's a fine lookin' filly, Major."

"All right," Devlin said. Before Charlie could thank him, he added a condition, as she'd known he would. "Now, why don't you show Simon here around town? There's still a couple of hours before the race."

"Oh, I'm sorry," she apologized, trying to sound sincere. "I've just been exercising Brandy, and I really need to bathe and change before I do anything else. Besides, I have a horse to buy, don't I?" Before her father could object, she added sweetly: "Don't go too far, Jim. I'll want you to back me up when we start dickering over a price."

She turned and hurried toward the staircase.

"Daughters!" said Devlin, watching her go. "Sometimes they can be more damn' trouble than a stud in heat!"

Jonah drove the old ambulance down toward Comanche Springs itself. The location was a large limestone waterhole surrounded by trees, a natural community camping ground for both Indians and whites heading west. Conestoga wagons were parked around one side of the waterhole, brightly painted tipis on the other. When they arrived, most people were still in town, enjoying the carnival, but a few older folks, or mothers and their children, had stayed behind to catch up on one chore or another. Some were even catching fish and soft-shelled turtles from the spring itself.

Sam found a clear spot for them and unhitched the team. Wordlessly, he led all three horses to the water and watched the colorful dragonflies as they skimmed across its surface. Jonah, meanwhile, opened the back of the ambulance, made a quick count and was pleased with the result. It had been a good day, and it wasn't over yet.

"Know how many bottles we sold?" he asked when Sam came back. "Thirty-eight! Couple more days like that, and—"

"How much we make?" asked Sam.

"Why, thirty-eight dollars, of course."

"How much is mine?"

"Well, under normal circumstances—"

"How much?"

"It *would* be nineteen dollars," said Jonah. "But let us not forget our overheads—that's expenses, to you, Chief. I had to buy a case full of whiskey, don't forget. And green chilies don't come cheap—"

"How much?"

Jonah cocked his head. "Well ... say, ten or eleven dollars."

"You put it in the save-box," Sam said softly. *"Now."*

"All right, Chief. Anything you say. But sometimes I get the impression you don't entirely *trust* me, and I can't help wondering why that is. I mean, aren't I a paragon of virtue, as honest as the day is long? Do I not wash behind my ears and say my prayers and—"

Sam had heard enough and started to turn away.

"Chief?"

Sam looked back.

"How long have we been partners?" asked Jonah. "Three years? Thereabouts?"

Sam shrugged.

"In all that time," asked Jonah, "have I ever given you cause not to trust me?"

Sam only stared at him, his eyes as unreadable as ever.

"Well? Have I?"

"Just put the money in the save-box," said Sam. "Now."

He himself went to some nearby shade, hunkered down and brought out five small, highly-polished animal bones. These he threw, dice-fashion, onto the sand before him. He studied the pattern they made for a long time.

"Oh, I see," called Jonah. "It's the bones again."

Ignoring him, Sam continued to study the bones and the way they'd fallen.

"Well, what do they say this time?" asked Jonah, approaching.

"The bones tell a story," Sam answered after a pause.

"I hope it has a happy ending."

"They say when Sam will return to his own people."

"Do they, indeed? And when will that be?"

Sam scooped up the bones, returned them to his pouch and continued to stare gravely at the dirt where they had fallen. "They tell a bad story. Say Sam will never return to his own people. Say I die here, instead."

Jonah licked his lips, the familiar need for a drink suddenly resurfacing in him. "Die? Here, in Texas? My friend, you're reading too much into what a bunch of coyote bones tell you."

"Hyena bones."

"Hyena, coyote, constipated wildebeest! It doesn't matter whose bones they are. The only thing that matters is that they can't tell a man's future!"

But Sam clearly didn't see it that way. "You are wrong. Bones don't lie. They tell the truth. Always."

He was so positive that his conviction left Jonah a little shaken.

"Well ... then you must have read them the wrong way, Chief."

Sam gave no indication that he had even heard Jonah.

Jonah stood there a moment longer, wanting to dismiss the message Sam had read in the bones but finding it easier said than done. At last he said: "I'm going back into town, lay down some bets while the odds are still good. You stay here and rest up, you hear?"

Still Sam appeared to be in a world of his own. Softening his tone, Jonah said: "And don't worry about what those bones say. After you win the race this afternoon, we'll both be rich! I'll have enough money to buy myself a saloon, and you'll have enough for passage back home to Africa."

But even as he said it, he had a sudden, uncharacteristically bad feeling it wouldn't turn out that way.

Chapter Seven

S am continued to ponder his fate for a long while after Jonah had gone, for there was no avoiding it once it had been foretold. And yet the premonition of his death did not concern him as much as the knowledge that he would never return to his homeland.

He sighed. He had not foreseen the way his life would go. How could he have? Few men even among the superstitious Zulus had such a gift. But he was here now, and it looked as if he would be here until death. Nothing could alter that. He had to accept it.

U-Shee-nah nickered as if sensing his sadness. He looked at her. She returned his look with eyes that seemed filled with compassion.

He had set up a rope corral close to a wild profusion of ocotillo bushes behind the ambulance. Now, on impulse, he rose and strode over to the marc. A few moments later he began to pluck crimson flowers from the thorny bushes and carefully braid them into the mare's silken black mane.

He was so absorbed in his work that he was entirely unaware when Charlie and Jim Prince entered the camping ground. Spying the horse, Charlie said excitedly: "Isn't she beautiful?"

"Now, don't go gettin' all lathered up, Miss Charlie."

"She *is,* though, isn't she?"

Prince had to concede that she was. "But remember," he added, "your father said you could only buy her if the price is fair."

"I know, I know. But you know my father. He thinks he's the only one alive who knows anything about horseflesh."

"An' you're out to prove him wrong, is that it?"

"I don't have to prove myself to anyone!" she snapped.

"Okay," he said softly.

At once she relented. "I'm sorry, Jim. That was my father talking, not me."

"Forget it, Miss Charlie."

"No." Impulsively she grabbed his arm, and though he struggled not to let it show, her touch electrified him. "You more than anyone don't deserve that kind of treatment. Sometimes I don't know how you put up with us."

God help him, he actually blushed a little. "Habit, I reckon."

"Well, don't ever change habits, Jim. I, for one, wouldn't want you any other way."

It was only after the words were out that she seemed to realize what she'd said. He looked down at her, sensing for the first time that he might actually stand a chance with her, but she turned away, her attention seemingly back on the mare.

"Come on," she urged. "Let's go buy ourselves a horse!"

Prince followed dutifully in her wake. "Be careful now, Miss Charlie. Remember, this feller ain't none too friendly. An' he's mighty quick with that spear."

At last Sam seemed to realize he was being watched. Turning, he saw Charlie and Prince coming and immediately scooped up his *assegai,* setting himself firmly between them and U-Shee-nah. Prince had been expecting something like that, and his right palm brushed meaningfully against the grips of his six-gun.

Charlie eyed Sam uncertainly and said, as if she were addressing some kind of dullard: "Hello. My name's Charlotte Devlin. This is my foreman, Jim Prince."

Sam only stared at them.

"Do you speak English?"

By way of reply Sam said: "What do you want?"

Prince glanced around. "Is the old man around? The doc?"

Sam shook his head.

"Where is he?"

Sam used the *assegai* to point off toward town.

"When, ah, do you expect him back?"

Sam shrugged indifferently.

Prince gestured toward the mare. "Know how much your master wants for the mare?"

Sam bristled. "No man is Sam's master."

Charlie tried a smile to reassure him. "Of course. We're, ah, sorry. We should have known. Is the mare yours?"

"U-Shee-nah belongs to Jonah. He won her with cards. A long time ago."

Charlie took a step closer, peered around Sam to study the mare. "U-Shee-nah. What a pretty name."

"She is not for sale."

"Well, now," Prince reminded him, "that ain't for you to say, is it?"

"U-Shee-nah is not for sale! Not ever!"

As he began to raise his *assegai* threateningly, Prince finally reached for his gun, but Charlie quickly stepped between them.

"Wait! Wait … what Jim here means is that the horse belongs to Dr Jonah. It's up to him whether he sells or not."

"Jonah never sell," said Sam. "Sam would never let him."

"Sam," she repeated. "Is that you?"

He nodded.

"We'd pay you well for the horse," she said, "maybe even a little more than she's really worth—"

"No money enough," Sam said in a low growl.

Charlie's jaw tightened. She was used to getting her way and that was how she liked it. But one look into Sam's bleak face told her that he wasn't about to relent. "Well," she breathed after a moment, "thank you … Sam. We won't trouble you anymore. Goodbye."

She pulled Prince away.

Sam watched them walk off, spear still raised. Then, when they were lost behind a stand of trees, he lowered the weapon and turned back to the mare.

Chapter Eight

Devlin and Harris were discussing land prices over drinks in the bar just off the lobby when Charlie and Prince got back. Devlin, spotting them from his corner table, gestured that they should join him, but Charlie ignored him and went directly to the desk instead, where she collected the key to her room.

As she hurried upstairs, Prince came into the bar and nodded thanks when Devlin told the bartender to fetch him a whiskey. "What's eating *her?*" the major asked.

"That filly," Prince replied, flopping into a chair across from him. "She's not for sale. Well, she *is,* I think. But the feller with the spear says he won't allow it."

Devlin raised his eyebrows. "A feller with a spear? What is he, some kind of Indian?"

"Some kind."

"And *he* won't allow it? A mite uppity, isn't he?"

Prince shrugged. "Maybe. But I'll tell you this much—they ain't sellin'."

Devlin stared thoughtfully into his drink. "Everything has a price," he said after a moment. "And if it makes my little girl happy, I'll pay it."

"But the Indian said—"

"Then we'll ask this other one, this doctor."

Prince pondered that. "I got a feelin' he'll tell you the same thing, major. Oh, he might *want* to sell—I seen him, he looks like he ain't never had more'n a few dollars at any one time in his whole life. Hell, he's so hard-up I hear he was peddlin' watered whiskey at a dollar a bottle this mornin', and right now he's down at the Crystal Palace takin' bets on this afternoon's race. Way I hear it, the Indian's runnin' in the race, an' Jonah fancies him for a winner."

Harris cleared his throat. "This ... friend ... of his is running in this afternoon's race?"

"Uh-huh."

"Then may I make a suggestion, Major Devlin?"

Devlin peered at him. "What is it, Simon?"

"If your daughter really wants that horse," Harris replied, sensing an opportunity to ingratiate himself with his host and, more importantly, his host's comely daughter, "then I suggest you abandon all talk of *buying* her, major. Let us talk, instead, of *winning* her."

J onah, by now in his cups, was indeed making bets with the patrons of the Crystal Palace Saloon. All the betting money was being held by a burly, black-mustached barkeep the locals trusted not to gyp them. The atmosphere was one of great excitement, for Jonah had used his gift of gab to arouse and excite his audience.

"I'll take ten of that," said one cowboy eagerly.

"Me too."

"Hell with that! Make it twenty, doc—your man ain't got a chance agin that Injun, Yellow Foot!"

In the midst of the activity, Major Devlin and Simon Harris pushed through the batwings.

The crowd melted away as the major led his companion to the bar. Jonah looked up fearfully, half-expecting to see Marshal McCabe again, and relaxed visibly when he saw only what he took to be two citified dandies.

"Taking bets on the race this afternoon?" Devlin asked casually.

"We are indulging in a little harmless wager, certainly," Jonah replied. "Would you care to join us, Mr. ... ah ... "

"I'm Major Devlin," said the rancher, and then, as if he didn't already know: "Who's your favorite?"

"Well, there are of course a number of possibilities. Some favor the Indian known as Yellow Foot. Others fancy a Mexican gentleman by the name of—"

"Who's *your* favorite?" Devlin repeated firmly.

"That, sir, is my good friend and colleague, the Chief. He can beat anyone you'd care to put up against him, as I expect him to prove this afternoon."

"Well, isn't that interesting," grinned Devlin. "You favor *your* friend—and I favor *mine.*"

"I'm sorry, Major?"

"My friend here, Mr. Harris. He'll be running in the race this afternoon, and I fully expect *him* to win."

"Save your money," Jonah advised. "The Chief can beat any man alive!"

"Is that a fact? Well, never let it be said that Lawrence Devlin was afraid to put his money where his mouth is."

Jonah raised his eyebrows. "How much are you prepared to *lose,* sir?"

Showing a deliberate flicker of concern, the Major turned to Harris and asked, loud enough for Jonah to hear him: "You're sure you can run fast, now?"

"Fast enough to whip any of these chaps," Harris replied confidently.

"Very well." And then, to Jonah: "What about … a thousand dollars?"

The saloon went dead quiet. It was an unheard-of amount. Jonah swallowed hard. "A … a *thousand,* you say?" he repeated weakly.

"That's right." Devlin stared him straight in the eye. "Unless of course you've suddenly gotten a little *snow* in your boots?"

Jonah hesitated. He turned, scooped up his glass and emptied it. His mind was whirling. He knew Sam couldn't lose. He *knew* it. But … Jesus—a thousand bucks? No, no he couldn't—

"Just as you predicted, Major," Harris said suddenly. "Nothing but hot air and cold feet!"

Stung, Jonah threw caution to the wind. "You're on," he said defiantly.

He and Devlin shook on it.

"I don't like to doubt any man's word, doc," said Devlin. "But you *do* have that kind of money to bet, I suppose?"

"Of course!"

Devlin knew he was lying. "Then neither of us has anything to worry about, do we?"

"Not a thing," Jonah replied with a confidence he no longer felt.

Apparently satisfied, Devlin swung around to the crowd and yelled: "Drinks are on me, boys!"

A cheer that almost raised the roof filled the drinking parlor as everyone crowded the bar.

B y the time Jonah stumbled into camp about an hour later, he was well and truly the worse for wear. Devlin had been a good host, whiskey had flowed freely and Jonah had certainly never been one to pass it up. Besides, once he realized the enormity of the wager he'd made with the rancher, he figured he needed something to calm his nerves.

As he'd leaned against the bar between drinkers, he'd tried to convince himself that Sam would win. 'Course he would! He'd never lost a race yet.

But suppose today was the day?

As one drink had followed another he'd thought about the way Sam had spent the previous evening, running with U-Shee-nah, using up all his stamina like he had more than enough to spare! You couldn't fault the Zulu for self-confidence. He believed in himself absolutely. But sometimes pride went before a fall …

That started him worrying even more. Suppose Sam was to fall, break a leg or twist an ankle? He didn't suppose the Major would call the wager off, he'd just say it was either an excuse or an act of God or some-such and still demand his thousand dollars. And he didn't strike Jonah as the kind of man who'd wait over-long for his money.

Almost before he knew it, Jonah realized he was drunk. But somewhere inside him, a part that somehow always remained sober told him he needed to get back to the camp and undress … compress … no, dammit, *im*press the importance of winning on his companion.

By the time his unsteady steps had led him back to the wagon, Sam was nowhere to be seen. Bleary-eyed, Jonah drew himself up irritably. Where was that man? He called Sam's name, but got no reply.

"Chief? Chief, where are you?"

Frowning, Jonah walked around to the far side of the wagon—and found Sam standing guard near the grazing mare.

"Hey!" Jonah slurred. "So, there y'are. Been lookin' everywhere for you."

Sam's eyes were flat and unreadable as he studied the lean, swaying wreck before him.

"Well," Jonah continued, "it's all set. Race is in th-thirty minutes an' every cent we got is ridin' on you. So—" He broke off, finally noticing Sam's glare. "What's wrong, Chief? Ain't *sick,* are you?"

Sam held his silence for a moment longer. Then: "A man and a woman come. They want to buy U-Shee-nah."

"Yeah? Who were they?"

"No matter! I tell them U-Shee-nah not for sale! They went."

Realizing how upset Sam was, and how important it was right then not to do or say anything that might distract him, Jonah nodded and clapped him on the shoulder. "Sure, Chief. Sure. You did the right thing." His gaze strayed to the mare and his frown deepened. He closed one eye as if that might make him see the animal more clearly. "Say, is that horse wearin' *flowers* in its mane?"

Sam ignored the question. "You must not sell U-Shee-nah. *Ever!* She belongs with Sam."

"Sure, sure. That's right, Chief. Now, why don' t you relax? Sit down. Rest yourself. The race is—"

"All you talk about is the race!" Sam said, frustrated. "The race is not important! U-Shee-nah is important!"

"Sure, she's imp … imp … what you said she is. But, so's the race. Can't you see that?" Impulsively Jonah grabbed Sam's arm. "Listen, Chief, you gotta understand somethin'. All the money we have is ridin' on your shoulders. If you win, we're rich. *Rich,* y'hear? But if you lose, well ... " His voice trailed off, because he didn't want to even think about the consequences. "So you see, Chief, you gotta win. You gotta!"

"Sam will win. Easy. No man can run with Sam. Not even other Zulus."

Cheered a little, Jonah said: "Attaboy, Chief! That's the spirit! Tell you what—you win this race, an' I'll *give* you the mare. How's that?"

For a fleeting moment something stirred inside Sam's eyes that might have been excitement. But it died almost immediately. He knew Jonah too well.

"You say this for true?" he asked suspiciously.

Jonah stuck out his jaw. "For true. All you gotta do is win."

"Sam will win."

He turned and walked back to the mare.

Chapter Nine

Gradually groups of excited locals and visitors began to drift away from the amusements to line the boardwalks on either side of Main Street, determined to get the best possible view of the much-vaunted foot race. The street itself slowly cleared. By the livery stable, Marshal McCabe and one of his deputies watched the contestants limber up and then take their positions. There were two young cowboys, a short, muscular Mexican, a long-legged Pomo Indian named Yellow Foot—and Simon Harris.

As yet there was no sign of Sam or Jonah.

Only Harris had dressed for the occasion. He wore a collarless white shirt with the sleeves rolled up to his bony elbows, his shirt tucked into baggy knee pants. On his feet he wore a pair of sand shoes he normally wore in lieu of slippers. Standing to one side of the other contestants, he seemed relaxed and confident as he performed a calisthenics routine that incorporated lunges, jumping jacks and squats. Pausing briefly, he waved at Devlin, Charlie and Jim Prince, who were occupying pride of place outside the Silver Spur Hotel.

The race was to be run over a distance of five hundred yards, in a more or less straight line, from the livery stable to the fort. There, the town officials had stretched a tape from one side of the trail to the other to mark the finishing line.

Harris was finishing his routine when he sensed a stirring among the onlookers. Stopping, he turned just as Jonah and Sam came into sight around the corner of the stable. Harris immediately recognized Sam as the man who'd raced against the stagecoach the day before—and went cold.

Now that he knew exactly who he was going up against, his confidence ebbed. No one liked the idea of losing at *anything,* of course, but there was more than just his pride at stake here. Harris had originally planned to win this race solely to impress the major and his daughter. The idea of winning this horse of Doc Jonah's had been his way of insinuating himself into Charlie's affections. But if he should lose to this muscular Zulu, then the major stood to lose a thousand dollars, and Harris himself considerably more than that in goodwill.

Distinctly worried now, he looked back toward the Silver Spur Hotel, and motioned for Devlin to join him. Muttering something to Charlie, the Major stepped down into the street and hurried over to see what Harris wanted.

Jonah watched the two men huddle together near the starting line, and wondered what they were discussing. Sam? It seemed a reasonable assumption.

"The Major's man over there," he said, thumbing at Harris. "You keep a sharp eye on him. This isn't the first race he's ever run in, an' everybody reckons he's good."

Focused on the route of the race, Sam ignored him.

"You hear me, Chief?"

"Sam hears you."

"All right then," Jonah said. "See you at the finish line."

Sam nodded.

Jonah hurried off to find a good place from which to watch the race.

Watching him go, Devlin muttered to Harris: "Don't worry about a thing. I'll handle it. You just make sure you run beside him."

Harris, his freckles standing out like spots of rust, nodded. Devlin gave him a parting clap on the arm and then hustled away.

Just then Marshal McCabe fired the shot to get everyone's attention. The crowd fell silent and looked at the lawman. The marshal moved into the street and faced the contestants.

"The rules are simple!" he said. "First man across the finishin' line is the winner! But I want a good, clean race here!

That means no jumpin' the gun, no pullin', no pushin', no holdin' the other man back! Got it?"

The runners muttered acknowledgement.

"All right!" said McCabe. "Runners—take up your positions!"

The contestants obeyed, toeing a line in the dust before them, setting their weight on one leg or the other and swaying back and forth to build the extra momentum needed to give them the best possible start.

Sam stood relaxed on the outside line on the opposite side of the street to the Silver Spur. Harris dutifully lined up beside him.

The marshal pointed his gun skyward. Before he could pull the trigger, however, he was interrupted by a commotion behind him. He turned and looked up the street. Several cowboys were pushing and shoving at each other about twenty yards from the finish line. There was no harm in them—they were just drunk, and it was less of a fight than a few good-natured high jinks. McCabe recognized Wes Rivers, Lon Cory and Rafe Hamblin, plus a few other men from neighboring spreads.

A couple of them went down in an impromptu wrestling match, raising dust as they rolled back and forth across the ground.

"Hey! You men! Get off the street!" yelled the marshal. "Go on! Get back out of the way!"

Slowly the cowboys stopped fighting and tried to help each other off the street. Their drunken antics made the crowd laugh—but try as he might, Jim Prince couldn't see the funny side. Impatiently he broke away from the group outside the Silver Spur and strode down the street toward them, gun in hand. As he closed in on the drunken cowboys, he fired several shots between their feet.

It had the desired effect, sobering them up fast.

"What're you men tryin' to pull?" he demanded.

"Nothin', boss," Rivers replied sheepishly, clapping his hat back onto his overlarge head. "We was jus' havin' some fun."

"Well, go have it someplace else!"

As the drunken hands stumbled away, Prince turned and waved to the marshal, signifying that the race could finally get started.

Again the crowd fell silent.

Jonah, having found himself a place in the crowd, took a quick pull from his flask. He then offered up a heartfelt prayer to whichever saint watched over drunks and fools, and crossed his fingers.

McCabe moved to the side of the street and again pointed his gun skyward.

"Runners! Ready … "

Each man tensely eyed his competition.

"Set … "

The contestants dropped to a crouch, leaned forward, braced themselves.

McCabe fired.

"GO!"

Almost as one the runners sprinted down the street, legs and arms pumping energetically as each sought to build a lead.

Harris quickly outdistanced the competition. Though he was nowhere near as graceful as Sam—who was bringing up the rear—he had power, and knew how to turn that power into speed.

Yellow Foot came up behind him, oiled black braids flapping, bare chest glistening, the fringes on his buckskin pants flying wildly as his long, muscular legs drove him on. The Mexican was in third place, but already beginning to tire and drop back.

One of the cowboys suddenly overtook him. His supporters in the crowd cheered and whooped. The second cowboy was also starting to tire.

And Sam was still trailing all of them.

The crowd was roaring them all on now, waving their arms, alternately cheering or jeering, depending upon whose performance they were watching, and whether it was good or bad.

Sam seemed unconcerned. He ran easily, without effort, but remained constantly a pace behind the last, trailing cowboy.

Jonah took another long swig of whiskey, thinking: *Lord, I hope he knows what he's doing ...*

Yellow Foot began to gain ground on Harris. Sensing as much, Harris glanced back at the Indian, then faced front again and kept going. The race was already past the halfway mark and Fort Stockton was coming closer with every long stride he took.

Suddenly there was a renewed roaring of the crowd. Yellow Foot looked back to see what had caused it—and saw that Sam was right on his tail.

The Indian dug deeper, put his head down and ran faster.

The crowd was going wild now. Harris chanced another look around just as Sam drew level with the Indian.

Any moment now the Zulu was going to start breathing down Harris's neck.

Harris pushed harder, lungs sawing painfully, pulses thumping in his ears.

Jonah drained his flask and shoved it back into his pocket.

Somehow Harris found an extra spurt of speed. The finish line was now almost close enough to reach out and touch.

Behind him, Sam overtook Yellow Foot.

Harris tried to shut out the cheering, knowing it was not for him but for the man who had started last and now looked like he was going to finish first. He continued to push himself. Sweat streamed down his face. His shadow raced along the ground before him.

Then—

A second shadow began to creep along beside it.

The Zulu!

Harris pumped harder. But no matter how much speed he summoned now, Sam was gaining ground with every pace he took.

Another yard vanished behind the Englishmen and Sam continued to close the gap between them.

Harris thought about what the Major had told him to do if it began to look like he might lose the race. He hadn't wanted it to come to this, but …

Sweat trickled into his eyes. He blinked, shook his head, kept running.

He thought about the Major, the Major's thousand dollars, the standing he would lose not only with Devlin but also with Devlin's daughter if he couldn't deliver the horse.

I've got to do it, he told himself.

Harris seemed to weave a little then, appearing almost but not quite to drift into Sam's path. But it had the desired effect; it made Sam slow a little so that they wouldn't collide … and it forced him in turn to swerve farther left, onto the still-churned dust where the Bar D men had been fighting just moments earlier.

The finish line came closer … closer … and Sam picked up the pace again, slowly but certainly gaining on Harris.

There was a sudden change in the roar of the crowd. It went up a notch. Hearing it, Jonah splayed the fingers of the hand covering his face and looked through the gap.

He almost collapsed.

Sam really was doing it! He was going to *win!*

He was now level with Harris and the two competitors were matching each other stride for stride. The large crowd was screaming for one man or the other, many jumping up and down or pumping their arms to urge them on.

Jonah, suddenly caught up in it, forgot all his misgivings and started yelling: *"C'mon, Chief! Run! RUN!"*

Sam burst into the lead, running effortlessly, while Harris started to falter. It looked to Jonah as if the race was in the bag.

Then Sam stumbled. He came close to falling but somehow kept on his feet. But it was too late—the damage had been done.

Harris sprinted past him toward the tape. Yellow Foot came right after him. Sam kept running but there was nothing elegant or graceful about him now—he was lumbering along, his face contorted as if in great pain.

Raising his arms, Harris burst through the tape with Yellow Foot a close second. Sam came in third and then the remaining runners straggled in. Immediately, Harris was surrounded by admirers and well-wishers.

Jonah, unable to believe what he'd just witnessed, watched numbly as some of the more exuberant townsmen hoisted the Englishman onto their shoulders. He thought, *That should be Sam up there ...*

But it wasn't.

It wasn't ...

As the full impact of what that meant finally struck home, he saw Sam hobbling painfully toward him. Trying to put on a brave face, Jonah went to meet him. "Here, Chief—lean on me. What happened out there, anyway? Cramp? I *told* you, Chief, you should've saved your energy last night—"

"Glass," said Sam grimly.

Jonah squinted up at him. "What?"

"Broken glass... in the dirt." Sam raised his injured left foot. The sole was scored with cuts and dust stuck to the blood.

Johan looked appalled. "Jesus, Chief. We got to get you to a doctor."

"You *are* a doctor."

"A *real* doctor, I mean!"

"No."

"But, Chief—"

"No doctor."

Jonah removed his high hat, scratched his thinning gray hair then dug a grimy handkerchief from his trouser pocket and handed it Sam to use as a bandage. "Well, we got to report what happened," he said. "That glass cost you the race."

And me a whole lot more than that, he reminded himself silently.

"Of all the lousy luck!" he went on. "We had that prize money in our pockets, and—"

"Luck had nothing to do with it," Sam said grimly. "There was *much* glass over where Sam ran."

Jonah scowled at him, not catching on immediately. Then: "You mean, someone … ?" It hit him then, and he looked at Devlin and Harris, who were surrounded by well-wishers. "Why, that dirty son of a—"

His words were drowned by a roar from the crowd as Devlin announced his customary: *"Drinks are on me, boys!"*

Everyone hurried toward the Crystal Palace.

Watching them go, Jonah said: "Can you make it back to the wagon alone, Chief?"

Sam nodded.

"All right. I'll meet you back there in a while."

"Where are you going?"

"To find the goddamn marshal," Jonah replied, "and tell him that someone fixed the race!"

Chapter Ten

It didn't take Jonah long to realize his mistake. Marshal Alexander McCabe just wasn't interested.

"But I tell you, it was *deliberate!*" Jonah exclaimed. He glared from McCabe to his elderly deputy, who was leaning indolently against one wall, drinking a cup of coffee. "Someone *deliberately* sprinkled glass in the dust where the Chief would run."

"Someone," McCabe repeated laconically. He leaned back in his chair, legs propped up on his desk. "And just who might that 'someone' be … ?"

For a moment Jonah was tempted to mention Devlin. But where was the proof? On the way here he'd recalled the drunken fight among the Bar D men. They could easily have used that as a distraction while one of them scattered the broken glass. But was that enough to link it to Devlin himself? He knew it wasn't. And in all honesty he couldn't say that Devlin had definitely put his men up to it.

But what about that hurried conference that Devlin had had with Harris before the race? What had Devlin been telling Harris? And right after that had followed a brawl that might not have been a brawl at all.

The more Jonah thought about it, the more he seemed to recall Harris swerving ever-so-slightly, in such a way as to push Sam directly into the path of the broken glass.

"How the hell should I know?" he replied at last. "One of the Major's men, I reckon, while they were—"

"Now, you hold it right there," McCabe snapped, bringing his legs down off the desk. "If you got proof to back it up, sure, I'll listen. But if this is just some kind of excuse … "

"What do you mean, excuse?"

"I've heard all about the wager 'tween you an' Major Devlin. Well, your boy lost—fair an' square, far as I could see. That means you owe the Major a thousand dollars. 'Course, if you was to cast doubt over the result … "

Jonah swelled up. "I am a man of *honor,* sir, and have never yet reneged on a bet! As the immortal Bard says, 'Life every man holds dear; but the dear man holds honor far more precious dear than life.'"

"Oh, come on, Doc, don't piss down my leg an' tell me it's rainin'. We both know what you are. You're a quack who sells watered whiskey and claims it can make a man act, feel and look half his age!"

It was on the tip of Jonah's tongue to add that it also worked wonders for the bowels, but then he realized what McCabe meant. In the eyes of the law he was indeed a somewhat less than credible witness.

"It's true I have no hard evidence," he admitted. "But Devlin's the only one who had anything to gain!"

"That's where you're wrong."

"Excuse me?"

"Me and just about half the town figured Yellow Foot couldn't lose."

"But that's different—"

"How?"

"Well … it … it just *is,* that's all."

"Like hell it is!" McCabe stood up and confronted Jonah. "The Major's an important man in these parts, doc. Real popular, too. So unless you got a witness—someone who actually saw one of the Major's boys plantin' that glass—well, I can't do nothin'."

Desperate, Jonah said: "There *is* one way we can settle the matter."

"I'm listenin'."

"You could always run the race over again, give the Chief a chance to prove—"

"No way I can do *that,*" McCabe said flatly. "An' even if I could, what good would it do? The way you say your man's cut up, hell, even Swifty Porter here'd probably beat him!"

Jonah sagged, knowing he was beat. "All right, Marshal, You've made your point. Good day to you, and thank you for your time."

"You leavin' town, Doc?"

"N-No. Just, ah, headin' back to camp, so's I can fix the Chief's foot."

The marshal nodded as if satisfied. But as soon as the office door had closed after Jonah, McCabe turned to his deputy and said: "Go find the Major, Swifty. Tell him I think his winnings are just about to run out on him."

When Jonah got back to the wagon he found Sam sitting on a rock with one leg crossed over the other, using the needle-sharp tip and sinewy 'thread' from an agave cactus to sew the deeper gashes in his foot closed. The Zulu was deep in concentration. He was also in considerable pain, but refused to let it show. Nor did he look up as Jonah's shadow fell across him.

"How's your foot, Chief?"

Finished stitching, Sam scooped up a handful of a leaf-and-mud poultice he'd mixed up and packed his injured sole. "It be better soon," he said.

"Good. Now, listen, Chief. We got to get out of here—pronto!"

"Why?"

"I'll explain later. Just help me hitch up the team."

He hurried to the wagon horses and set about preparing them for travel. But he was so nervous that his fumbling fingers couldn't manage the task.

Sam eyed him suspiciously. He then limped over to Jonah, wordlessly brushed him aside and hitched up the team.

Jonah guiltily hurried away, gathered their gear and threw it into the back of the ambulance.

"All set?" Jonah asked after Sam had cinched the last strap and bridle.

Sam nodded.

Jonah pulled himself up onto the wagon seat. "Then get up here and let's make dust!"

"Why?" Sam asked.

"I told you."

"You told me you would tell me later."

"That's right. And I *will*. Later."

Sam fetched U-Shee-nah and tied her to the tailgate. It seemed to Jonah that he had never seen Sam work slower.

"Come *on,* Chief! Quit fooling with that damn' horse and get up here!"

Sam ignored him. When he'd finished, he picked up his *assegai* and limped around to the front of the wagon. He was just about to join Jonah on the seat when Jim Prince and three riders rode into the campsite.

Realizing that Jonah and Sam were leaving, the Bar D foreman rode slowly up to the wagon. Behind him rode Cory, Rivers and Hamblin, their hands hanging ominously close to their gun-butts.

Sam, seeing them and automatically thinking that Hamblin was here to continue their earlier fight, immediately raised his *assegai* in warning.

Ignoring him, Prince reined up beside Jonah. "Goin' somewheres, Doc?"

Jonah shrugged and tried to look innocent. "Why, uh … no, of course not!"

"Glad to hear it," said Prince. "I reckon the Major will be, too, seein' you still owe him a thousand dollars."

"I h-haven't forgotten," Jonah said. "Why, did not our own beloved Thomas Jefferson once say that—"

Prince's eyes went flat. He dismounted and held up one hand to Jonah. "The money, Doc. A thousand dollars. Then you can be on your way."

"Sure." Jonah started to reach down under the seat.

The Bar D men instantly pulled their guns.

"Easy, Doc," Prince cautioned. "Bring them hands out real easy."

Jonah obeyed. In his hands was a small metal box.

Sam stiffened, recognizing the box in which Jonah kept their savings. "No!"

Prince, hearing the anger in the Zulu's voice, drew his Colt and leveled the weapon at Sam. "Better tell him to drop that spear, Doc, 'fore I let a little daylight through him."

Unable to meet Sam's eyes Jonah said: "Do as he says, Chief."

"But that our *save*-box! All of Sam's money in it!"

"Please, Chief. Do like he says."

Knowing he had little real choice in the matter, Sam lowered but refused to drop the *assegai.*

Prince turned back to Jonah. "All right. Bring the box down here, Doc."

Jonah obeyed, slowly climbing down from the wagon.

Prince holstered his gun, took the box, opened it and quickly counted the money inside.

"This ain't no thousand dollars," he said when he was finished. "Not even three hundred, by my tally." He closed the lid. "Makes you about seven hundred shy."

"A temporary state of affairs, I assure you," Jonah said. "But I have no intention of leaving the debt unpaid. That is not my way. Why, anyone'll tell you that Dr Quincy Martin Jonah is as straight as a wand. That his word is inviolate—"

Prince cut him off. "The Major's headin' back to his ranch, Doc. He wants his money *now.*"

Jonah glanced away from him and murmured something.

"What was that, Doc?"

"I don't have it."

"Then it looks like the Major was right, don't it? He figured you'd try an' gyp him, first chance you got."

"I'll pay him when I'm in funds."

"And when will *that* be? Sometime never?"

"I am more than happy to sign a promissory note—"

"I'm sure *you* are," said Prince. "But the Major prefers cash. And he'd like it *now,* Doc."

"Well, as I just explained, I don't have it. I don't know where that leaves us, but—"

"It leaves *you* in serious trouble," Prince growled. He began ticking off his fingers. "Peddlin' watered whiskey around town... lettin' your, uh, 'friend' here attack one of my men before witnesses... tryin' to run out on a debt that you just so happen to owe to the most important man on the Pecos. I mean, way I see it, things are gonna go awful hard for you. Major Devlin'll see to that."

Jonah remained grimly silent, not knowing what to say in his defense.

"But I got good news," Prince continued.

Jonah brightened. "Y-You have?"

"Sure. The Major's daughter's taken a real likin' to your mare there, an'—" Prince paused as Sam stiffened, then added: "—an' she figures the animal's worth close to a thousand, so—"

"It's a deal, sir!" Jonah exclaimed. He avoided Sam's glare, allowing desperation to override any sense of obligation he had to the Zulu, and at the same time hating himself for his weakness.

"Fine," said Prince. "Then I'll be takin'—"

Sam stopped him. "No! U-Shee-nah is not for sale!"

"Quiet," Jonah said. "I'm sorry, Chief, but I don't have any choice."

"It's agreed, then?" said Prince.

"Agreed!" Jonah said—then stopped, cold, as the point of Sam's *assegai* suddenly pressed against his windpipe.

Startled at just how fast Sam had moved, Prince took an involuntary step back, then jerked his iron, warning: "Drop it, mister, before—"

Again Sam moved with unbelievable speed, slamming the flat-side of the blade down across Prince's gun-hand. The blow numbed Prince's hand and the gun dropped from his suddenly-numbed fingers.

"Damn you!" he exclaimed.

A lot of things happened very quickly then.

Instinctively, Cory triggered a shot at Sam. The bullet gouged a ragged furrow across the Zulu's left shoulder. But Sam was already on the move, this time stabbing Cory with the *assegai.* Cory screamed and collapsed, clutching a bloody shirtsleeve.

Simultaneously, Sam saw Rivers and Hamblin bringing their own guns up. He darted in close, struck first one man alongside the head and then the other with the flat of the blade. Rivers collapsed, all but unconscious. Hamblin's hands went to his already-tender face and Sam hit him again, this time with his fist. Hamblin buckled.

Teeth clenched, Prince reached down with his good hand and tried to scoop up his fallen Colt.

Impulsively, Jonah crowded him and brought a knee up into his face, yelling: "Run, Chief! *Run!*"

Sam hesitated, loath to leave the mare.

Jonah and Prince continued to grapple, but there was never any doubt as to who would win the contest. Prince, the stronger man, managed to get his finger through the trigger guard and the somehow gun went off in the struggle. Jonah howled as the bullet seared his leg, but still he clung to Prince.

"Go on!" he shouted at Sam. "For God's sake, Chief, run before they lock you up!"

These were the magic words. They reminded Sam of the slavery from which he had once escaped and had sworn never to endure again. He took one last look at the mare, then turned and raced off into the surrounding trees.

Prince struck Jonah alongside the head with the butt of his gun. Jonah sank to the ground, unconscious. Prince fired two shots after the fleeing Zulu, but he was firing left-handed, on the fly, and missed.

Prince whirled, took a step toward his skittish horse with the intention of going in pursuit. But then he saw that Cory needed medical attention and Rivers and Hamblin were both still crawling around on their hands and knees.

"Dammit!" he snarled. Turning to the handful of onlookers who, upon hearing the shots, had gathered nearby, he snapped: "One of you! Go get the doctor! And the marshal, while you're at it!"

Chapter Eleven

Jonah had no recollection of how he ended up in Major Devlin's suite at the Silver Spur. For a long time his world was just black and silent. Then came a shock of cold water splashing him in the face and all at once he was sitting up in a ladder-back chair in the middle of a plush looking suite, coughing, spluttering and fighting for lost breath.

It all came back quickly then. The sight of the dark bruise on Jim Prince's right hand assisted recollection.

Pain did its bit, too. A big lump on the side of his skull throbbed violently, and when he reached up to examine it, he winced, for it was tender to the touch. As for his left leg … He suddenly remembered that he'd been shot—or at the very least, bullet-scored. When he looked down, he saw that the leg of his pants had been slit at the seam and someone had bandaged the wound.

Finally he looked around the room. Devlin and the Englishman, Harris, were standing beside a tray of drinks, the Major smoking a cigar, Harris nursing a whiskey. Jonah saw the marshal there as well, but that was cold comfort. He might represent the law in these parts, but he'd already made his feelings clear where Jonah was concerned. And he was unquestionably one of Devlin's many toadies.

Jonah knew he'd get little help from McCabe.

Lastly, he saw Devlin's daughter, Charlotte, seated by the window, her expression speaking eloquently of her uneasiness with the entire situation.

Prince returned the empty water glass to the tray and Devlin approached. It was then that the trial—for that's exactly how it seemed to Jonah—began.

Jonah listened until he couldn't keep quiet any longer. "Now wait a minute, Major. I keep telling you that the Chief didn't mean any real harm. Believe me, if he'd wanted, he could've just as easy killed your men. Instead he just … just *incapacitated* them. In defense of his own life, I might add!"

"So you say," Devlin said smoothly. "But my men tell a different story. They say the Zulu attacked them for no good reason."

"He had every reason! They were going to shoot him, just like your man here shot me!"

"That was your own doin'," said Prince. "If you hadn't tried to wrestle me, you wouldn't have gotten shot. Anyway, it's only a flesh wound."

"Which makes it a very lucky day for you, sir, else I would have seriously considered bringing charges against you!"

"Go ahead. See what it gets you," Devlin said.

Jonah, knowing the Major was right, calmed down. "In any case," he went on, "the Chief was only trying to protect his property—his share of our savings. He knew nothing about our wager. He just figured your men were trying to steal what didn't belong to them."

Charlie spoke at last. "I accept that. But the mare … that *wasn't* his property. He told us that himself."

"But in a way it *is* his property, Miss—Devlin, is it? You see, I promised to give Sam the mare if he won the race and—"

"But he *didn't* win," snapped Devlin.

Jonah looked up at him. "No. But he would have, if some kind gent hadn't buried broken glass in his path."

"Glass?" said Prince, eyes narrowing suddenly. "What're you talkin' about?"

Before Jonah could reply, Devlin said: "Now that you mention it, Doc, I *did* hear something about your man having an accident."

"It *wasn't* an accident," Jonah said pointedly.

Charlie got up and came over. "Surely you're not accusing my father of deliberately injuring your friend?"

Jonah turned to the girl, about to say yes, he sure was. But then he remembered where he was—in enemy territory, so to speak, with said enemies all around him.

"I say," Harris said, his voice sounding strangely lacking in conviction, "what rotten luck. I thought your chap had pulled a muscle or something."

"Same difference," Devlin pointed out. "Either way, he lost." He turned to face McCabe. "The important thing here is that you find that savage and punish him for chopping up my men."

"I'm way ahead of you, Major," McCabe replied. "My deputy's out roundin' up a posse right now."

"But, Major—" Jonah began in alarm.

"Save it. I could have you arrested for obstructing justice, you know. Isn't that right, Marshal?"

"Just say the word."

Devlin appeared to consider that for just long enough to make Jonah squirm.

"There's no need for that, father," interrupted Charlie. "After all, I *do* have the mare, which discharges this man's debt. And none of the boys were seriously hurt."

Devlin glanced at Prince, who shrugged. "She's right, sir."

Devlin considered briefly. "Very well," he said at last. "You're fortunate that I am a merciful man, Dr Jonah. You're free to go just as soon as you sign that mare over to me. And never show your face in this territory again, or you might not find me so forgiving next time."

"And … and the Chief?" asked Jonah.

"A man attacks Bar D men without any justification, I'm afraid I can't overlook that." Devlin turned to McCabe. "You find that damn savage, y'hear?"

"Don't worry, Major. He's as good as in jail right now."

He nodded politely to Charlie and then lifted Jonah out of his chair by the scruff of his neck. "Come on, you. You can sign the bill of sale the Major's got ready for you and then make tracks."

After they'd gone, Charlie stood up and looked from the foreman to Harris. "Will you excuse us for a moment? I'd like to talk to my father alone."

Devlin raised one eyebrow, but nodded when Prince looked his way. "Escort Mr. Harris out to the ranch, will you, Jim?"

"Yes, sir."

As the door closed behind them, Devlin said impatiently: "All right. What is it, Charlie?"

She held back a moment before saying: "Dr. Jonah *is* wrong, isn't he?"

"About … ?"

"The glass … his friend getting cut. It *was* an accident, wasn't it?"

"Of course."

"Will you swear to that?"

Devlin's face hardened. "What kind of a question is that?"

"I just want to be sure—"

"And you won't just take my word for it?" When she didn't answer he said: "You'd better watch what you say around me from now on, young lady. Remember, none of this would've happened if you hadn't been so all-fired set on owning that mare."

"Then you *did* have that glass planted in the street!"

"Of course not." With effort he managed to bridle his anger and softened his tone. "Sweetheart, let's not argue. You *know* I had nothing to do with that, and frankly I'm hurt that you believe I could have. I mean, we've had our differences in the past—that's only to be expected between two headstrong people—but surely I've been enough of a father for you to know I wouldn't stoop so low as to injure a man just to win a race or collect a few paltry dollars?"

She didn't answer.

"Well, haven't I?"

"I'm sorry," she said at last. "Of course you have."

But much as he wanted to, he couldn't miss the hollowness with which she said it.

Chapter Twelve

The mood around town was high. Everyone had enjoyed the first day of the carnival and most of the men were thrilled by the idea of joining the posse. By the time Marshal McCabe reached his office a group of some thirty mounted men were waiting for him. He eyed them briefly, recognizing some, frowning over others, whom he guessed had come in off the surrounding ranches or were just passing through. They were all armed and eager to go.

"I take it Deputy Porter here has told you all about the man we're goin' after," McCabe said. Then as everyone nodded: "Well, the plan is to take him alive, if we can. But he's a fighter—he proved that this morning, cuttin' up one feller and clobberin' two more. So if he shows any resistance when we run him to ground … well, we'll just have do what we have to."

He was about to start toward his horse when someone from the back of the crowd called: "Marshal?"

McCabe narrowed his eyes. "It's … Ramsay, isn't it? What's your problem, son?"

"No problem. But shouldn't we … we be sworn in or somethin'? You know. To make it all legal-like?"

He had a point. But there was no time for that now. McCabe said: "All right. All of you raise your right hands." Then as they obeyed: "Now say, 'I swear.'"

There came a chorus of *I swears.*

"Consider yourselves deputized," said McCabe. "Now let's ride!"

They'd barely left Fort Stockton behind them when McCabe saw Jonah's ambulance wagon rattling along ahead. He led his men around the vehicle without slowing, and left Jonah coughing in their dust.

Hauling rein, Jonah rose to his feet and yelled: "Go ahead! You'll never catch him! Not the Chief! He'll run you and those damn horses of yours right into the ground!"

He would have said more, but the dust was chokingly thick. Sitting back down, he reached into his jacket. Only one thing could cut that dust now—and it came in a refilled hip flask.

It had been a hell of a day, and he was hoping the whiskey might ease his troubles. He missed Sam badly. There were times when the Zulu was a royal pain, but that was only because he cared. In some ways they were like a father and son. It was just that sometimes it was difficult to know who was supposed to be whom. He had taken Sam in, taught him English, and the ways of the white man. But there were plenty of times when Sam had taken care of *him,* too.

Jonah might be many things, but *stupid* wasn't one of them. He remembered all the camps they'd made when he'd drunk too much and fallen asleep right where he was. There hadn't been a single time when he hadn't woken up the following morning to find that Sam had covered him with a blanket against the night chill, and bundled something under his head for a crude pillow.

They were good together, and good for each other. But now it looked as if their partnership had come to an end.

He couldn't blame Sam. He, Jonah, had known how much the mare meant to the big Zulu. He shouldn't have been so ready to give it up in order to pay his debt. But he'd never been what you might call a courageous man. That Major, Devlin, he would have taken the debt out of his hide, no doubt about it. So Jonah had had to do something.

Still …

You betrayed your friend, he told himself miserably. *You promised him that mare, and you broke your promise.*

Of course, it wouldn't be the first time Jonah had ever done that, but he'd never yet broken a promise to anyone who'd meant anything to him.

He cursed bitterly. For once the answer to what ailed him could not be found in whiskey. Instead of easing his troubles it only made him feel more depressed.

He looked around, examining his surroundings, hoping to find Sam out there somewhere, watching him. He'd wave, Sam would wave back, come down and join him, and it would be like it had been only a few short hours before. He'd tell Sam how sorry he was about the way things had panned out, how he'd make it up to him … but what chance would Sam ever give him now?

He was the only friend you ever had, you know, he thought. *The only friend you're ever likely to have. Won't ever be another Chief …*

"Goddammit!" he groaned. "Where in hell *are* you, Chief?"

The answer was: *Not far.*

Assegai in hand, Sam watched him from a perch high in the rocks to the south … and didn't like what he saw.

Or rather, what he *didn't* see.

U-Shee-nah.

Could it be that the one called Jonah really *had* parted with U-Shee-nah? But he had *promised* …

Suddenly the word tasted sour in his mouth, and he told himself he had been a fool to ever believe anything that Jonah had said. What was a man's word worth when given to someone like him? It should have meant everything. But he had come to this country as a slave, and as much as he hated to admit it, he had been little more than a slave to Jonah. He could see that now.

He turned away and limped painfully down off the slope until he reached a sheltered bowl of land where he had built a small, smokeless fire surrounded by small flat rocks. His left shoulder ached, too, where Cory's bullet had scored it. But that was the least of his concerns just then.

He used the point of the *assegai* to stir up the embers, then sat down and unwrapped his injured foot.

As the poultice fell away, he saw that the crude stitching had broken and the worst cut had reopened. No matter. There was another way to seal the wound.

He looked at Jonah's kerchief. Now it was only a reminder of the man who had betrayed him. Impulsively he threw it into the fire and watched the flames consume it, and consume too whatever feelings he had held for the old man.

At length he used the *assegai* to drag a stone from the fire and turn it over. Smoke rose from the blackened underside. He stared at the stone, preparing himself for the pain to come; then, without hesitation, he set his wounded foot down on the rock.

His teeth clamped hard. The urge to take his foot off the rock was almost impossible to resist, but somehow he managed it. Sweat ran down his face, into his eyes, but still he stoically bore the pain. At length he peeled his foot from the stone, examined the burned sole and saw that he had, as he had hoped, cauterized the wound.

Much as he wanted to go after U-Shee-nah now, he knew he had to give his foot a chance to heal, perhaps a day, perhaps two. Reluctantly, then, he threw dirt on the fire to kill it, then leaned back against the rocks and waited for his world to stop spinning.

Chapter Thirteen

Three nights later Sam approached a small ranch that sat at the mouth of a rugged canyon. In the darkness it was little more than a cluster of buildings, outbuildings and corrals, with pasty light showing at some the tarpaper windows of what he took to be a cabin and a bunkhouse. He had no idea whether or not the ranch belonged to the man called Devlin, but if it did, then this was where he would find U-Shee-nah.

As soon as he could, he had gone in search of her. In the cold, dark hours before yesterday's dawn, he had returned to Fort Stockton and searched one livery stable after another for the mare, but she was nowhere to be found. By the time the sun peeked over the horizon, he realized that Devlin had already left town and taken the mare—*his* mare—with him.

That left him with only one other course of action. He must scour this land until he found Devlin's ranch, for that was where he would find U-Shee-nah. And he knew he would never know peace without the mare. He and U-Shee-nah were kindred souls. He could hardly comprehend the connection himself; it just *was.*

Slowly, carefully, Sam approached the ranch, moving in silent stealth from one patch of cover to the next. Around him, a cool breeze carried with it the sound of cicadas. The main corral stood behind a tall barn, and a few horses were clustered together in one corner, asleep standing up.

Moving quickly despite his injured foot, Sam went up and over the corral fence, into the corral itself. Wakening, the horses stirred and a couple of them whinnied softly.

Sam addressed them quietly in Zulu. The horses calmed a little, but remained bunched together, as if for protection. He approached them slowly; saw that U-Shee-nah was not among them. He slipped inside the barn, checked the stalls and emerged dejected. But U-Shee-nah was out here somewhere … and he would not rest until he found her.

As he returned to the fence, one of the horses—a roan—broke away from the rest and followed him. After a few yards he felt its velvety muzzle nudge at his bare back, and turned.

The roan watched him through large, liquid eyes. A second later it whinnied and shook its head.

Sam reached for the horse's big head and stroked it. As he did so, the moonlight showed him the faint scars that still lingered around his wrists, and all at once memories came flooding back; of the chains he had been forced to wear on the long voyage from his homeland, and the beatings and whippings he and the others had taken for no reason that Sam could ever understand, except a perverse nature that made one man want to hurt another.

The memories, still so vivid, engulfed him completely, and for that one brief moment in time he was oblivious to all else.

Then he became aware of the roan watching him. He looked from the horse to the other horses, huddling in the corner of the corral, and realized that they were every bit as much slaves to the people of this ranch as he had been to the master of his plantation.

He turned again. Beyond the corral fence was freedom—nature's gift to all.

His mind made up, he trotted to the gate and quietly swung it open, then urged the horses toward it. Already spooked by his presence, they needed little encouragement. They cantered past him, through the gate, out onto the waiting plain. Sam, smiling for the first time in days, jogged after them, pleased with himself.

These were cow ponies, however, and accustomed to being near the ranch. After only a short distance they slowed and began to graze.

Sam jogged closer, frowning. He was giving them freedom. Why were they not taking it? Could it be that they were *happy* here? That their owners treated them *well?* From his own experience he could hardly imagine such a thing.

The roan was still watching him. Sam paused beside it, spoke softly in Zulu. The horse pricked its ears, and when Sam continued on toward the distant mountains, the roan went after him.

One by one the others followed suit … until he had his own herd trotting dutifully behind him.

When he realized the horses were following him, he turned to look at them. The horses stopped and began to graze again. A flicker of pleasure stirred Sam's stern features as he realized they were following him now because they *wanted* to. They *wanted* to be near him. They *wanted* him to lead them.

They were *his.*

Something moved in him, a feeling that this was what *he* wanted, too; to be among these creatures, the only living things he felt he could trust and among whom he knew contentment.

He nodded to himself, and then turned, *assegai* in hand, and loped toward the mountains.

The horses followed.

Over the next week Sam continued to scour the territory for U-Shee-nah. He and the herd holed up in the high country during the daylight hours and went in search of the mare after dark. Though he never found her, the Zulu seldom left a ranch without its stock following behind him, adding to his herd.

He never questioned his dominance over them. It was simply the way it was. And like any stallion, he looked upon the herd as his family, a family U-Shee-nah would join, as soon as he found her.

It was this thought, and the unswerving bond of loyalty he received from the other horses, that consoled him in the cold, dark hours after midnight, when he wondered where his mare was, and hoped she didn't think he had abandoned her.

One night the barn of Vern Hinkle's Rocking 7 burst open and the ranch horses exploded into the yard, raising dust everywhere. Within half a minute the hands came tearing out of their bunkhouse, some half-dressed, others still pulling on boots and pants. For a while there was only chaos. Horses thundered this way and that. Men yelled and shouted in confusion. Dust roiled everywhere. And then ...

Then the horses were gone into the night.

One bow-legged cowhand swore savagely as he slammed his hat down into the dust at his feet. "Dammit! It's like tryin' to catch a ghost!"

"'T'ain't no ghost what's stealin' them horses!" growled another. "It's that damn' Shadow Horse again!"

Neither did it stop with ranch-stock.

Two nights later a bunch of grazing ponies were stampeded away from a sleepy Caddo Indian village. No one ever saw what caused the stampede. But folks could speculate, and *did.*

It was Shadow Horse. Who else *could* it be?

One humid afternoon two cowboys were driving a small herd of wild mustangs through a narrow channel that fed into to a box canyon when a large rock came bouncing down the westernmost slope. As it gathered momentum, it triggered a miniature avalanche that separated the men from the horses. No one ever knew for sure why that rock chose just that moment to roll, but the mustangs got clean away.

Much as it didn't like to be forced into action, the Fort Stockton Cattleman's Association finally posted a thousand dollar reward for the capture of the outlaw stallion known as Shadow Horse. After two more ranches were hit and the stock run off never to be seen again, the reward rose to two thousand. Men loaded guns and went hunting what they still thought to be a rogue stallion ... but at the end of every hunt they always dragged their weary bones back home empty-handed.

Slowly but steadily the reward posters spread across that part of Texas. Doc Jonah even came across one nailed to a tree growing beside a much-traveled trail.

"Must be one hell of a shadow, is all I can say!" he decided after he finished reading it. And then, because he'd grown accustomed to talking to himself in Sam's absence: "'The light of lights looks always on the motive, not the deed, the shadow of shadows on the deed alone.'"

Then he flicked the reins and the old wagon rattled on its way.

Chapter Fourteen

Major Devlin stood on the porch outside his home at the Bar D and studied each of the men before him. There were three of them, and he knew them all to one degree or another. They owned and operated ranches throughout the territory, and they were here now as spokesmen for themselves and every other rancher who'd been hit by Shadow Horse.

Devlin had heard them out. That was the least he could do. But beyond that he didn't see that he could be of much help. So far Shadow Horse had left him alone. Presumably even that beast knew better than to pit itself against the might of the Bar D.

He'd said as much, but the angry delegation that now confronted him couldn't, or wouldn't, see things that way, and that irked Major Devlin.

"But it *does* concern you, Major!" said a long-faced, dark haired man named Will Maddox. "It concerns all of us! That big white devil hit my place last night, run off every head I own, and—"

"White?" echoed Vern Hinkle. *"White?* Why, you near-sighted ol' fool! That outlaw ain't white, he's dark gray. I—"

"Red, he iss, by God!" said the big, bearded Swede, Karl Olander. "Red ass fire, and—"

"Never mind what color he is!" snapped Maddox. "Point is, gents, that outlaw's got to be stopped! An' right away, too, 'fore he bankrupts all of us. Dammit, he's worse than the Comanches!"

Vern Hinkle nodded in agreement. "An' lessen you want to lose your brood mares some dark night, maybe even Brandy,

God forbid, you'd better start helpin' us hunt that stallion down, Major!"

Devlin's mouth tightened at the corners. Around him, hands were decorating the ranch for tonight's party. It was his birthday and he wanted to celebrate it in style. After all, it wasn't every day a man turned fifty. Besides, he knew that such gatherings had their uses. You could meet and possibly influence important people in such a relaxed setting—that's why he'd invited the new governor, Richard Coke, and the Republican senator, James W. Flanagan, to be guests of honor. Business could be discussed, deals made, introductions solicited.

All of which underlined one undeniable fact: Devlin was the biggest and most important rancher thereabouts, and it was a position he liked because it brought with it a measure of respect and deference among the lesser ranchers. He didn't like it when they forgot their position and started treating him as an equal, and making demands. He was about to remind them that a man caught more flies with honey than vinegar, when his attention was taken by a rider who came racing through the gate.

Devlin recognized Wes Rivers and wondered what had set a fire under the man. The cowboy made no effort to spare his horse as it crossed the yard and when he finally reined it in, the animal made an ungainly sliding stop that sprayed dust everywhere.

"We got him, Major!" Rivers exclaimed breathlessly. "We got Red Eye!"

That caused a stir among the ranchers, for Red Eye was well known to them—a big albino stallion that had roamed wild and free for as long as folks could remember, and whom Devlin himself had long wanted to capture, break and then use as a potential breeder.

"Jim an' the boys are bringin' him in now!" Rivers said. "Along with about thirty head!"

Some of the tension ebbed from Devlin and he allowed himself a smug smile as he surveyed the other ranchers. "Well, now, boys, I reckon that solves all your problems."

Maddox scowled. "How d'you figure that?"

"Well, with Red Eye in captivity, you shouldn't lose any more stock."

"Major," said Hinkle, "you ain't tryin' to tell us that Red Eye an' Shadow Horse are one an' the *same,* are you?"

"Why not? Red Eye's been running off our stock for years now, so—"

"But Red Eye's an albino! I seen him myself, lots of times."

"So haff I," said Olander. "And I seen Shadow Horse, too, by God! And he ain't even *close* to being white. He's red ass—"

He broke off at the sound of approaching horses. Everyone turned as Lon Cory and a few other Bar D hands drove a herd of wild mustangs toward the corral area. There were two corrals, each rectangular and divided down the middle by a seven-foot fence. Cory rode out ahead, opened the gate that led into the empty corral with the tallest fence, then hurried out of the way as the rest of the crew drove the herd inside.

Prince and Rafe Hamblin brought up the rear. They had the albino, Red Eye, securely roped between them. The stallion tugged and pulled, snorted and tried to charge them every step of the way, his fury seemingly boundless.

Once they had him in the corral, they quickly removed the ropes and rode back through the gate, leaving Cory to secure it behind them.

"Come on, fellers," said Devlin.

He led his visitors across the yard until they could all peer through the corral slats and watch as Red Eye stormed around the perimeter, knowing it was too high to jump and slamming himself broadside against the rails in an effort to shatter them.

Prince, who had already had his fill of the stallion, dismounted and walked up to Devlin. "I'm gettin' too old for this, Major."

Devlin laughed. "That'll be the day!" Unexpectedly, he reached out and pumped Prince's hand enthusiastically. "Good work, Jim! I think this calls for a celebration. C'mon, boys!"

He led everyone into the house. Last to enter were Hinkle and Maddox. They took one final look at Red Eye and then Maddox spat into the dust.

"Still say that ain't Shadow Horse," he grumbled.

"You an' me both," Hinkle agreed. "An' I got me a feelin' it won't take the Major long to find it out."

In the adjoining corral, meanwhile, Charlie's horse Brandy and four mares watched Red Eye as he continued to rear and toss his head and throw himself at the fence. Brandy pranced skittishly, clearly unhappy with the presence of a potential rival. A cowboy who'd been forking hay from a wagon into the barn loft stopped and grinned at him. "Easy, feller. The Major ain't gonna let no wild stud get near your fillies!"

But Brandy wasn't so sure, and whinnied.

Sharing his misgivings, one of the mares in the far corner answered him.

It was U-Shee-nah.

S am had been sitting cross-legged beside a water hole, alternately drowsing in the midday heat and watching his herd as it drank or grazed.

Suddenly he froze and listened intently. He wasn't reacting to anything he'd heard so much as something he'd sensed. He had no explanation for it, but he knew better than to ignore the feeling. There was a sudden restlessness in him, something that went far beyond his usual disquiet. But what had caused it?

He felt it was U-Shee-nah.

Picking up his *assegai,* he rose to his feet and scaled a steep, nearby slope as easily as if he'd been climbing stairs.

The summit overlooked a spacious, verdant valley, at the far end of which stood a sprawling ranch that he had not yet had the chance to visit. He had intended to check out the spread after dark.

Now, as he looked at the place, he could barely resist the urge to go down there right now. But that would be madness. The darkness was his ally. Like it not, he had no choice but to wait for the sun to die.

Chapter Fifteen

After the delegation of ranchers had enjoyed Devlin's fine whiskey and even finer cigars, they mounted up and rode off. Devlin watched them leave then spent a moment looking at the approaching dusk before saying: "What do you really think, Jim?"

Prince, hat in hand, studied his profile. "About what, Major?"

"You reckon Red Eye and Shadow Horse really *are* one and the same?"

"I'll be honest with you, sir—I don't know. Maybe."

Devlin had been hoping for something more definite than that. As it was, Prince's doubts seemed to confirm his own.

"Better have some of the boys keep watch for the next few days," he said.

Prince nodded. "What about Brandy? You want a special watch kept on him?"

"No," Devlin replied. "Just make sure he's locked up in the barn each night."

"Okay. But he ain't gonna like it, Major. 'Specially now he's got competition."

They both turned to Red Eye, who was still testing the fence in search of a weak spot while the rest of his herd looked on.

"Maybe not, Jim. But it's for his own good. What with the party and everything tonight, I don't want to take a chance on Red Eye getting loose and mixing it up with him. As big as Brandy is, he'd be no match for that albino."

"I'll see to it," said Prince.

They descended the porch together, Prince heading for the bunkhouse, Devlin toward Brandy.

The horse saw him coming and trotted over to greet him. Gleaming like a new penny, he meant everything to Devlin. He came close enough to touch. But when Devlin tried to pet him, the horse made a sudden, skittish crab-like movement to put himself out of reach and continued prancing on around the corral. Devlin laughed, because that was one of Brandy's favorite tricks.

"So this is what grown men do when they should really be running their ranch—playing with horses!"

Devlin turned, his smile widening as his daughter came to join him.

"Ah, but Brandy's no *ordinary* horse," he pointed out.

"Well, you're right about that."

"What are you doing out here, anyway?" Devlin asked. "I thought you were keeping our British friend company."

Charlie made a face. "He's no friend of mine, Daddy, and he never will be."

"Now, don't take that attitude—"

"Daddy, the man's a bore! And worse than that, he's full of his own self-importance. All he ever seems to talk about is himself."

"Perhaps that's because he's trying to *impress* you."

"And why would he want to do that?"

"You're no longer a child," Devlin reminded her. "You're a woman now—a handsome one. Time you started thinking about your future."

"I don't have to think about it. I *know* what's in my future. This place."

"But what about a husband? I'd appreciate some grandchildren one of these days, you know."

"No you wouldn't. They'd make you feel old, and I suspect that fifty is about as old as you're prepared to get. In any case, when I marry—*if* I marry—it'll be for love. Not position."

"What does that mean?"

"You may think you're a wily fox, but I can see right through you, Daddy. You'd like nothing more than for me to marry your aristocratic English friend and maybe inherit a title. 'Lady Charlotte Harris'! It would be good for business, wouldn't it? Add some respectability."

"I thought I was already respectable enough."

"You are. But I know you. A little extra can't hurt. Well, I'm sorry to disappoint you, but I can't stand the man, much less consider him as marriage material."

"Well, you're going to have to decide sooner or later. You don't want to end up on the shelf."

"When I find the right man, I'll marry."

"Just not to Simon?"

"Not in a million years!" she said, and laughed.

Devlin looked at her. That was her opinion now, he thought, but after he'd worked on her a little more, she'd change her mind. There were worse things in life than privilege, respectability and comfort. Perhaps she needed to be reminded of that.

"Come on," he said, putting an arm around her and leading her back to the house. "We're supposed to be holding a party here tonight. Time you and I got ready for it."

By early evening the Bar D had been transformed. Streamers and lanterns hung everywhere, and the air smelled of hickory wood fires, pit-barbecued beef and the finest wines and spirits. Guests had come from everywhere to celebrate Devlin's half-century, and the yard was crowded with buckboards, small wagons and a scattering of saddle horses.

The sounds of chatter and laughter blended with the clinking of glasses. The gay music of a Mexican four-piece band drifted through open windows to travel on the cool night breeze. Inside, several couples were dancing, among them Simon Harris with a less-than-enthusiastic Charlie, while

Devlin himself seemed to be everywhere at once, but always paying special attention to his more influential guests. In one corner, and trying to be as inconspicuous as possible, Jim Prince fussed at his string tie, uncomfortable as always when he had to wear his Sunday-go-to-meeting suit. The rest of the hired men clustered around punchbowls a few feet away, more or less enjoying a party of their own.

Outside, one of the hands who'd been stuck with night-watch wandered slowly along beside the corrals, a rifle tucked under one arm. When the music finally reached its climax there was enthusiastic applause from the audience. The night-guard, whose name was Vaughan, paused and looked enviously at the house. Somewhere in the darkness behind him, Red Eye gave a defiant snort.

Vaughan turned. "Weren't for you," he growled, "I'd be inside right now, havin' me a high time."

He turned his back on the stallion and continued walking. Inside the house the band struck up another tune … and in the deepest shadows of a corral corner post not twenty feet away, Sam slowly rose to his full height.

He peered into the corral. Sensing him there, Red Eye charged in his direction, only to veer off at the last moment.

Sam shrank back, deciding that it was unlikely that U-Shee-nah would be in the same corral as these wild mustangs. That left only the adjoining corral and the barn beside it.

There was a sudden rattling of chain. It reminded Sam of times he would sooner forget. But when he looked toward its source, he saw that it was only the night-guard, making sure the barn door was properly fastened. Satisfied that it was, he walked on toward the bunkhouse.

Sam broke cover and ran quietly to the adjoining corral. His sudden appearance scared one of the mares there and she whinnied and shied away from him. Sam immediately dropped to his stomach and froze.

In the bunkhouse doorway the night-guard, Vaughan, turned back to survey the ranch. Seeing nothing unusual, he leaned his rifle against the tie-rail and started rolling a smoke.

Sam watched him a moment longer, then turned to the corral, and his heart jumped. Because there, on the other side of the corral, U-Shee-nah stood eyeing him.

For a moment he thought he'd imagined her. Then, realizing he hadn't, he quietly climbed over the fence into the corral.

Although his presence alarmed the other mares, U-Shee-nah greeted him as he had hoped she would. She came close, draped her head over his shoulder and pulled him close as if hugging him.

There were no words to describe how Sam felt at that moment.

Then reality returned. He had found what he sought. Now he must get her away from this place.

He started toward the corral gate, knowing that the mare would follow him. But by now the other mares had bunched together before him. He waved the *assegai* to clear a path to the gate. As he did, the iron blade caught and reflected in the moonlight, and one of the mares panicked and cow-kicked the fence.

In the quiet it sounded like an explosion.

Over by the bunkhouse Vaughan immediately straightened up in alarm.

Sam dropped to the dirt and lay there. In the darkness he could sense the guard looking at the corral, wondering what, if anything had spooked the horses.

Finally, Vaughan picked up his rifle and started for the corral, intending to take a closer look for himself.

Sam rolled under the fence, out of the corral and hopefully out of the guard's sight.

"Easy now, gals," Vaughan shushed. "Easy ... "

Before he could say more, there came a loud whinny from inside the barn—Brandy.

Red Eye immediately answered Brandy's challenge.

Vaughan stopped. "So that's your problem, uh? Can't decide which—"

Sam rose up behind him and, hands clasped, clubbed him at the base of his neck. Vaughan grunted, his finger instinctively tightening on the rifle's trigger as he lurched

forward. The long gun roared, shattering the silence. But the night-guard didn't go down. Though dazed, he turned, cursing, levered in another round and fired at Sam.

The bullet missed and before Vaughan could fire again, the Zulu jumped him. Both men slammed against the corral fence, Vaughan wincing as a rib cracked. He never got a chance to recover. Sam punched him in the face and this time the night-guard went down and stayed down.

By then, though, it was too late; the alarm had already been raised.

Chapter Sixteen

Devlin jerked open the ranch house door and light spilled onto the covered porch ahead of him. He raced outside, followed by Prince and a bunch of alarmed guests, all anxious to know what was happening. Fearing a Comanche attack—something you could never rule out in those parts—Devlin and Prince had armed themselves with rifles and now stood crouched on the porch, trying to see in the darkness beyond them.

By now Sam had opened the corral gate and run inside. Waving his arms, he yelled at the mares to run, knowing that only in confusion could he and U-Shee-nah hope to escape.

Spooked by the gunfire, the mares poured out of the corral and started galloping in all directions. In the adjoining corral, Red Eye threw himself against the gate, determined to shatter it and join the mares in their freedom.

Inside the barn, Brandy heard both the mares and Red Eye. He reacted angrily, neighing shrilly and kicking at the walls of his stall.

By the light of the porch lanterns Devlin saw Sam and U-Shee-nah bursting out of the corral and opened fire on the Zulu. Prince did the same. But in all the chaos their shots went wide.

Even as they tried to correct their aim, they heard a sudden, loud splintering of wood. Whirling around, they saw that Red Eye had finally shattered the gate and was bursting out into the night. The albino reared up and pawed the air, screaming triumphantly as the rest of his herd poured through the opening around him, adding to the confusion.

The horses tied up along the porch hitch-rail immediately started pulling and plunging nervously, until their combined weight ripped away the railing and supports.

As the porch overhang collapsed and the guests scattered to avoid being crushed under it, lanterns fell and shattered, splashing kerosene-fed flames everywhere. Some caught on the upholstery of Governor Flanagan's jump-seat phaeton and the wall-eyed horse in the traces panicked and broke into a run, hauling the burning, brake-locked vehicle along behind it.

Above the screams of the alarmed guests, Prince yelled to the hands that had come stumbling out of the bunkhouse: *"Get some water! Hurry! Put these fires out!"*

Sam, meanwhile, hurriedly led U-Shee-nah away from the corral—only to find Red Eye blocking his way.

Seeing him as a rival, the albino charged him, determined to trample him underfoot. Sam quickly vaulted over the corral fence to avoid the stallion's attempt to kill him.

He landed awkwardly on his injured foot and his leg went out from under him. By the time he'd scrambled up, Red Eye was herding U-Shee-nah and the other mustangs off into the night.

No!

Sam was about to leap back over the fence and go after them when he glimpsed movement out the corner of his eye. He turned—just as the burning phaeton came toward him, lurching perilously on its wheels. At the last moment the horse pulling it swerved to avoid a collision. The shaft broke, allowing the horse to get away while the vehicle itself continued on until it crashed into the fence, spewing flames everywhere.

The impact broke one of the spindly wheels and it rolled toward the barn, igniting scattered hay along the way. Within moments the barn was also aflame.

Sam looked at the chaos he had inadvertently created. He had not meant for any of this. But all that mattered now was U-Shee-nah—and turning away from the blazing ranch, he loped off after Red Eye and his herd.

Oblivious to Sam's escape, Devlin, Prince and the hands were using their jackets to beat out the fire on the porch when Devlin heard Brandy's fear-laced whinnying. He turned toward the barn, eyes widening in horror.

The barn was in flames!

Panicking, Devlin jumped off the porch and sprinted across the yard. Seeing him go, Prince raced after him, pointing toward the corral troughs as he yelled: *"Everyone! Get a bucket-brigade goin'! Hurry!"*

By the time Devlin and Prince reached the barn they'd been joined by Charlie, her face screwed up in anguish as she heard Brandy screaming inside. Covering her face with her arm, she started to go inside—but Prince grabbed her and hauled her back.

"Don't be a fool! You're—!"

He broke off as Devlin plunged recklessly up to the flaming barn and desperately tried to unlock the chain that kept the doors closed. Letting Charlie go he barked: *"Stay here!"* Heedless of his own safety he raced after Devlin, yelling: *"You can't go in there, Major! It's too late!"*

But there was no reasoning with Devlin. All that mattered now was Brandy. He looked at Prince, so distraught he didn't even recognize him. And when Prince tried to pull him away, the rancher swung wildly at him.

Prince went down, mouth bloodied. But, loyal to the end, he scrambled up and again tried to drag the rancher away. *"No, Major! Get back! Get back!"*

Frantic, Devlin twisted loose, flung the chain aside and disappeared into the flames.

Inside, the barn was like a furnace. Hot air seared Devlin's lungs. He could barely breathe, but still his only thought was for Brandy.

He looked around. Brandy's stall was empty. Where was he? He tried to yell Brandy's name but all that came out was a smoky rasp. Then, through the flames, he saw that the doors ᵒᵗ the back of the barn had been kicked open. Hope surged through him. Had Brandy somehow managed to escape into the night—?

A burning crossbeam suddenly fell from above, crushing Devlin face down on the hay-strewn floor and trapping him beneath it. At once fire from the beam spread onto Devlin's clothes, burning through to the skin of his arms and legs, then his face, and he started screaming.

A moment later Prince reached him, the foreman's own face smoke-blackened. Half-choked by the smoke, he yelled: "Hold on, Major!"

Ignoring the pain as best he could, he grabbed one end of the beam and, face twisting, lifted it enough for Devlin to scuttle free. The flames had spread everywhere and the rancher was aware only of one thing—unendurable pain.

Prince dropped the beam. As it slammed to the hay-strewn floor more fire sprayed everywhere. Avoiding it, he went after Devlin, tried to hold him still while he scooped handfuls of dirt over the flames.

It was easier said than done. In a world of his own now, Devlin tried to fight him until Prince, in desperation, punched him in the face. Only then did Devlin go limp, leaving the foreman to tear off his jacket and beat out the remaining pockets of fire.

What was left of the Major when he'd finished wasn't pretty.

Indeed, it was downright *awful.*

Dawn found the skeletal remains of the barn still popping occasionally and sending lazy tendrils of smoke into the sky. The ranch itself was draped in silence. Nothing moved. Nothing remained to hint that this had been the scene of a celebration only hours earlier. The front of the house was fire-blackened, the porch just a charred memory. The corrals stood empty, save for one horse—Brandy—who had trotted back in of his own accord, just ahead of that day's sunrise.

The guests had long-since departed, chief among them Simon Harris. The Englishman had said he didn't want to be a burden to them at such a time, but Charlie knew that what he really meant was that he'd feel a whole safer in Fort Stockton. All she asked him before he left was that when he got there, he summoned the army surgeon.

He did. And upon his arrival at the Bar D, Captain Aaron Curtis had gone to work on Major Devlin for two hours solid. Now the heavyset, balding medic opened the parlor door with a weary sigh and went inside. At once Charlie leapt up from the sofa with Prince beside her, their expressions speaking adequately of their concerns ... and fears.

The doctor's eyes moved to the liquor cabinet and, taking the hint, Prince went over and fixed him a little medicinal.

Charlie said: "Is he ... will he be ... ?"

"He's sleeping right now," answered Curtis.

"But he'll be ... all right?"

"He'll *live,*" Curtis said carefully, taking his drink.

"What does that mean?"

"I'm afraid there'll be some disfigurement," the doctor explained. "His right arm... right leg and of course ... his face."

Charlie sobbed and Prince quickly put his arm around her to hold her steady.

"Be strong, Miss Devlin," the doctor continued. "Nowadays there are some reasonably successful procedures for the remodeling of malleable flesh being practiced back East that might possibly ... disguise the worst of it. Of course, he won't be able to undergo anything like that for a while. What he needs right now is peace, quiet and rest."

Charlie seemed unable to speak, so Prince said: "Thanks, Doc. Can you, uh, show yourself out?"

"Sure. But I'll be back later this afternoon to check on him."

After the doctor had gone, Charlie said: "Some birthday present."

Then she started to cry.

Prince drew her to him, holding her with a tenderness she had never suspected.

"It's all right," he assured her. "It's all right ... "

For a long, painful moment she sobbed into his chest. Then she felt him pull away from her, and when she looked up there was something in his expression that scared her.

"I'm gonna find that murderin' savage, Charlie," he promised her. "I'm gonna find him an' bring him back here, alive, so the Major can have the satisfaction of watching the sonofabitch *hang!"*

Chapter Seventeen

Late that afternoon, the tracks Sam had been following led him to a small canyon. He stopped in the entrance and his herd halted behind him. About three-quarters of the way along the canyon there lay a large natural pool around which a mixture of horses drank and grazed.

One of them was U-Shee-nah.

The grullo mare stopped drinking, raised her head and looked at him. A moment later she began trotting toward him.

Standing watch on a rocky ridge overlooking the pool, Red Eye swung his big, bone-white head around. Seeing Sam and sensing the challenge in him, the albino stamped, whinnied angrily and raced down to cut the mare off. When she wouldn't obey, Red Eye bit at her flanks in an attempt to make her return to the herd.

U-Shee-nah avoided him nimbly and kept heading for Sam.

The stallion reared up and bellowed a defiant challenge. Sam squared his shoulders and glared at the albino to show he wasn't afraid. Then he began jogging toward U-Shee-nah.

Red Eye watched him come, angrily stamping the ground.

Halting, U-Shee-nah divided her attention between the two, knowing what must inevitably follow.

Sure enough, Red Eye charged.

He came racing toward Sam but Sam forced himself to stand his ground, knowing from experience that this would be nothing more than a bluff—an attempt to scare him away rather than do battle.

Red Eye came nearer. The ground trembled beneath Sam's feet. His teeth clenched, but still he stood there, staring the stallion right in the eye—

Twenty feet out the albino suddenly turned to one side, and Sam let go a relieved breath. Red Eye stopped, reared up, flashing his hooves. Still Sam refused to move, raised the *assegai* and started to slowly, slowly circle the stallion, taking a course that would bring him closer to U-Shee-nah.

Seeing as much, the albino charged him again, figuring to cut him off. Again Sam planted himself where he was; again Red Eye wheeled away at the last moment.

The canyon wore a cloak of silence. The mustangs watched the competition from one end, Sam's herd from the other. Again he started moving. Again Red Eye charged, but this time it was no bluff, and Sam knew it. He waited till the last possible moment and then threw himself aside. He hit the ground, rolled on his bullet-scarred shoulder, came up with the *assegai* still in hand and prepared to meet the stallion's next attack.

He didn't have to wait long. Red Eye flung back his head and then came at Sam full-tilt. Again Sam dodged aside, but this time he couldn't avoid Red Eye entirely. The horse clipped him as he charged by, and twelve hundred pounds of pure muscle sent him crashing to the earth.

Red Eye wheeled, sensing victory, reared again, came back in. Sam rolled and kept rolling, somehow avoided those flailing hooves. Finally he jumped up, covered in dust, grabbed the *assegai* and saw the albino come charging at him again.

This time the Zulu ran at the stallion, face contorted with rage as he screamed, *"Ingonyama! Ingonyama! INGONYAMA!"*

I am lion!

Having an enemy charge him, was a new experience for Red Eye. And having no idea how to deal with it, the albino veered away, ran in a tight circle, shaking his head, snorting, unnerved and reluctant to acknowledge it.

Sam ran at him again. *"Ingonyama! Ingonyama!"*

This time Red Eye held his nerve. He charged in, big teeth snapping as he tried to injure his opponent.

Sam backpedaled, weaved, and somehow kept out of the stallion's way.

The fight for survival went on for ten more minutes. Charge, retreat, counter-charge, a brief skirmish that left neither combatant badly injured. But now Red Eye's charges were neither as fierce nor as quick as they had been. He was reevaluating his foe.

But the fight had to end, and soon. And there could be only one winner. Red Eye understood this, even if he didn't understand the nature of this human who was challenging him. As the stallion prepared for a final charge, Sam set himself, *assegai* raised, and waited for the albino to attack.

Finally the stallion charged. Sam braced himself, knowing he would have one chance to use the short stabbing spear, and he had to make it count.

But even as Red Eye came blurring toward him, hooves slamming the earth, spraying dust and stones behind him, Sam knew he couldn't kill such a noble creature—a creature that was obeying its instincts, even as he was obeying his own.

At the last moment he thrust the *assegai* into the ground and stood with arms at his sides and big hands open, fingers flexing.

Red Eye loomed ever-larger before him—

—and at the last moment Sam sidestepped, twisted, leapt and grabbed the albino around the neck.

Red Eyed, caught off-guard, did all he could to dislodge the human being clinging to him, but Sam resisted the albino's every attempt to shake him loose.

Red Eye fought on. He swapped ends, reared, balled out and sun-fished, and still Sam kept his arms locked and his face pressed against the albino's neck.

Red Eye continued to fight, but now Sam started hissing words between each tortured breath. *"Cweba ... cweba,* white one ... *zola ...zola* ...Be calm ...be calm as the sky... "

For several more minutes the stallion fought him. But now he was beginning to show signs of exhaustion.

Sam was equally spent. What had started as a contest to be settled by brute strength was ending as a battle of wills.

At last Red Eye was too weary to continue. The sweat-lathered stallion slowed to a stop, took in great, weary snorts of air, and stood there, muscles trembling.

Sam held on, unwilling to let go in case the stallion still had some fight left in him.

"Zola ... zola ... " he said hoarsely. And then: *"Ngqotsho."*
It is finished.

He finally released Red Eye and stood back, ready to move the instant the stallion started fighting again. But the horse had nothing left. He stared at Sam as if trying to figure out this strange human enemy.

Deliberately, Sam turned his back on the stallion and strode over to U-Shee-nah. As he rubbed her head and allowed her to nuzzle at his sweat-and-dust-caked chest, he murmured to her in his own language.

Red Eye watched them, his head lowered in defeat.

When Sam was sure that he had made his point, he pulled his *assegai* from the ground and walked with the mare toward the waiting herd.

Still Red Eye watched, not moving.

Sam broke into an exhausted jog. U-Shee-nah trotted after him.

Red Eye watched her go but made no move to stop her.

Obediently the remainder of the herd fell in behind Sam and the mare, until all that remained in the canyon were the wild mustangs ... and after a long look at Red Eye, even they turned, in twos and threes, and went after the Zulu.

Beyond the canyon lay a wide, dry arroyo. Sam led his herd across it. They formed a magnificent procession perhaps fifty or sixty strong.

Red Eye wearily followed some hundred yards behind.

Chapter Eighteen

Jonah had no sooner entered the town of Little Spring when he saw the reward poster tacked outside the town constable's office. The thing that drew his attention was the sketch that accompanied the wording. It was a better than passable rendering of Sam.

The poster itself offered:

$10,000 REWARD
FOR INFORMATION LEADING TO THE CAPTURE OF THE
OUTLAW
SHADOW HORSE
ALIVE!

Jonah looked at the poster for a long while, his expression pained, his conscience even more so.

What have you gone and done now, Chief? he thought. *I knew I should've gone after you! Dammit, I'm the only one can look after you out here!*

He thought some more about how he'd been so ready to let Major Devlin have U-Shee-nah even though he'd promised her to the big Zulu. Giving her to Devlin had gotten him off an unpleasant hook. But had he stood his ground and called the Major's bluff, had he said no and kept his word and given her to Sam ... well, he'd still have Sam as a friend. And his conscience wouldn't be half as troubled as it had been ever since.

Got to find him, he decided at last. *Got to find him and somehow get him back to his own people. If I don't do that, I won't know a moment's peace ever again.*

His mind made up, he snapped the reins with new purpose. The ambulance wagon lumbered in a wide circle and then headed back toward the Pecos country.

Chapter Nineteen

"It's like the ground opened up and swallowed the sonofabitch," grumbled Wes Rivers.

It was now a week after the fire and Prince and the Bar D hands had been scouring the territory for Shadow Horse ever since. But the Zulu had left no trail behind him; and even if he had, this country was so big they could probably search it for a year or more and still never find him. Why, he might even have left the territory altogether by this time.

But that was something Jim Prince doubted. He sensed that the Zulu was still holed up in these parts somewhere. He wasn't about to leave without that mare he'd set so much store by. And if he *was* still out here somewhere, Prince was going to find him—and make him pay for what he'd done.

"All right, Wes," the foreman replied, crossing his hands over his saddle horn. "You an' the men head back to the ranch… get fresh horses an' start lookin' again."

A low moan went through the riders behind Rivers.

"Boss," Wes said wearily, "me'n the boys been out since daybreak. We're *beat.*"

"Don't argue!" Prince barked. "Either you continue lookin' or pick up your wages!"

Prince and Rivers eyed each other for a long beat. There had always been mutual respect between these men, and they'd never fought once in all the years they'd known each other. But ever since the fire Jim had become a changed man, and Rivers didn't cotton much to the change.

Still, Wes knew there was no point in arguing with the foreman. Jim was hurting because Miss Charlie was hurting, and they all knew how he felt about *her.*

With a resigned shrug Wes turned to his men, said: "You heard the boss. Let's ride."

He spurred his horse away, and the others followed. Prince watched the search party ride off then he finally led his own men in the opposite direction.

It was late afternoon when he saw something in the far distance that made him think his luck was changing.

"What the hell *is* that, boss?" asked Lon Cory, squinting to see it clearer through the heat-haze.

"Only one thing that color in these parts," Prince replied. "It's Doc Jonah's wagon."

The ambulance wagon was still a long ways off, but Prince was right—its bright yellow color made it stand out like a bright star on a dark night. And if Doc Jonah had come back into the territory, deliberately flouting the Major's warning to the contrary, there could only be one reason.

Prince thought fast and then turned to Cory and Rafe Hamblin. "Get down there," he said. "Follow him, but don't let him see you. I ain't sure yet what he's up to, but odds are he's headin' for Shadow Horse."

Cory looked doubtful. "He's also headin' into Comanche country, 'case it's escaped your notice."

"I don't care if he's headin' into hell itself!" grated Prince. "You'n Rafe, here, stick with him. See if he'll lead you to the Zulu."

"An' if he does?"

"Then one of you ride back to the ranch an' let us know. I'll take it from there. Now, move out!"

In foul mood, Jonah camped early that evening, built a small fire and then settled beside it, staring into the flames as he worked hard and diligently at getting good and drunk. Tonight, however, the whiskey didn't help. 'Fact, ever since the Chief had gone his own way, it had helped less and less. Indeed, if things didn't change soon, he was in real danger of turning temperance.

Jonah was just drifting into an uneasy slumber when he heard the snapping of a deadfall branch somewhere out in the darkness. A moment later he heard what sounded like the braying of a mule—but by then he'd snatched up his rifle and was staring into the night.

"All right!" he called. "I know you're out there, whoever you are! Best you come in friendly, because I know how to use this thing!"

"Whoa, there!" replied a husky voice. "No need for that! I'm peaceable."

"Then come ahead and prove it."

There was more crackling of underbrush, and then a skinny, prematurely-aged man in a grease-stained, ankle-length duster came shuffling into the firelight, leading a pack-mule in his wake. Thinning white-blond hair straggled from beneath a high-crowned, wide-brimmed hat pulled low, and his hollow cheeks were covered by a patchy beard the color of wheat. He had watery eyes, a thin beak of a nose, a mouth that was all but hidden by his unclipped soup-strainer mustache.

"If you'll overlook my candor," said Jonah, "who the hell are you?"

"Name's Everett Cooper. An' you'd be … ?" He squinted up at the wagon. " … this here, Doc Jonah, I reckon?"

"Indeed I am, sir."

"I saw your fire," said Cooper. "Figured you might welcome some company."

Jonah nodded, suddenly remembering a quotation he had once used on Sam and U-Shee-nah, and which now seemed peculiarly fitting to his own situation. *When people are lonely they stoop to any companionship.*

"Sure," he replied. "Sit down, Mr. Cooper." He didn't miss the way Cooper's rheumy eyes lingered on the bottle beside him. "Drink?"

"Now, that is right charitable of you, partner." Cooper took the bottle, downed a long belly-belching swig. "Thanks. Man gets mighty dry up in the high country."

"You never said a truer word." Jonah gestured to the mule. "A prospector, I see."

"Yep."

"Know these mountains well?"

"Like I was born in 'em. Ain't no gold around here, though, if that's what you're figurin'." He drank again. "An' even if there was, I ain't sure I'd wanna stay an' find it—not after what I seen today."

"Oh?"

"If I *did* see anythin', that is," Cooper muttered. "An' I ain't entirely sure I did."

"How do you mean?"

The prospector studied Jonah. "Maybe *you'd* understand, at that."

"Excuse me?"

"Said you were a doctor. Well ... as a doctor, d'you reckon a man can see things that ain't truly there? If'n he's been alone too long, I mean?"

"It's possible, yes. Why? What is it you thought you saw?"

"It was this mornin'. Me'n Miss Maude—that's my mule, here—we seen a herd of mustangs bustin' out of this canyon, an' ... an' ... "

"Go on."

"Well, leadin' 'em," said the prospector, "runnin' along jes' like he was a hoss hisself, was this great big black feller."

Jonah felt a sudden tingle of excitement, but kept his tone casual as he said: "Did you, indeed. And, ah, where exactly was this, Mr. Cooper?"

"Near Blue Mountain. They was headed into Blanco Canyon, which is Comanche territory, else I would've followed." He paused and cocked his head at Jonah. "Reckon you figure I'm loco, huh?"

"I didn't say that."

"'Mean you believe me?"

Jonah shrugged noncommittally. "Like you said, if a man's alone too long in these isolated wastes, his mind can play some peculiar tricks on him. For that reason I, ah, wouldn't mention this to anyone else, if I was you."

With a nod, Cooper stared moodily into the fire. Jonah eyed him thoughtfully, then asked with studied casualness: "This, ah, this Blanco Canyon you mentioned. How far is it from here?"

"'Bout ten miles, I reckon."

"In which direction?"

"West." Cooper's eyes sharpened suddenly. "You ain't thinkin' of goin' in there, are you?"

"Probably not. But if I *did,* and I was to see the same thing *you* saw … well, I'd be able to corroborate your story, wouldn't I? Set your mind at rest."

"What's co-robber-what you said?" asked Cooper.

"I could *confirm* it. Prove that it wasn't your eyes playing tricks on you."

"Well, it's your funeral, Doc. But, like I say, Blanco Canyon, that's Comanche country. Lot of white men have gone into it, but precious few have ever come back out again."

In the darkness beyond Jonah's campfire, Cory's teeth flashed in a brief grin. Turning to Hamblin, he said: "You better make dust. Jim'll want to know about this, soon as possible."

Hamblin nodded. "You gonna follow the old man?"

"Hope to tell you."

"Well, if'n you do, you be sure an' watch out for them Comanch' tomorrow."

"Count on it. I ain't about to let anyone creep up and lift *this* child's scalp."

Chapter Twenty

The Bar D was slowly starting to look like its old self when Hamblin rode his lathered horse up to the ranch-house and slid from the saddle. A new section of roof now overhung the porch, and work had already started on erecting a new barn. But that was one thing about the Major, Hamblin reflected, as he stamped up onto the porch and let himself into the house. The man never did let weeds grow under his feet.

When Hamblin entered the dining room, he was exhausted from his all-night ride. Devlin and Charlie were halfway through breakfast. The Major sat at the head of the long table, handling his silverware awkwardly because of his injured, gloved right hand.

When he looked up, and Wes saw the full extent of his injured face, it was all he could do not to flinch. Once a handsome man, the right side of Devlin's face now looked as if it had been stretched tight across his skull. The injury made his right eye and the right side of his mouth hang lop-sided. The fire had taken off his mustache and eyebrows and left his olive skin crisped and blistered. What was left of him now was a cruel caricature of what used to be. And though he had recovered better than anyone expected, it was impossible to know how the fire and his injuries had affected his mind.

Devlin listened quietly as Wes made his report, then thought aloud: "Blanco Canyon's a full day's ride from here. Maybe more … " Because of his burned lips his voice had become slightly slurred, and sometimes Charlie and Prince had to struggle to decipher what he was saying. "Have every available man saddled and ready to ride in fifteen minutes, Jim. And saddle a horse for me!"

Charlie frowned at him. "Daddy, you're in no fit state to ride yet."

Ignoring her, Devlin said: "You heard me, Jim! *Move!*"

For once Prince didn't obey. "I don't know, Major," he said hesitantly. "Miss Charlie's right. You can't ride like—"

"Don't tell me what I can and can't do, damn you!"

Prince cast a helpless glance at Charlie, who said: "Daddy, you've only been out of bed a few days."

Ignoring her, he stared angrily at Prince and softly: "I gave you an order, Prince. Either carry it out or collect your damn' time!"

Prince bridled, but held back a retort. A pleading look from Charlie helped. Through his teeth, he said: "Yes, Major. 'Bout how far we expectin' to ride?"

"Far as it takes to catch that murdering bastard!"

Prince turned and headed for the door, accompanied by Hamblin. "I want extra horses for every man," Devlin added. "The best we have!"

"Yo!"

As the two men left, Devlin seemed to shrink a little, fatigued but refusing to admit it.

Charlie waited until the door had closed before saying: "Daddy, how *could* you treat Jim that way? It'd serve you right if he *did* quit on you."

"What're you talking about?"

"You had no right speaking to him that way and you know it. Not after all the years he's worked for you, been your friend."

"Mind your own business, Charlie. This has nothing to do with you."

He could see she was going to pursue the subject, and he was too tired and too sick with pain to indulge her. Abruptly he snatched up his cane—he'd learned to hate the thing because it made him feel more like an invalid than he already was—and lurched to his feet, then began to walk unsteadily toward the door.

Charlie jumped up and brushed past him.

"Where d'you think you're going, young lady?"

"With you, Daddy."

"You're not going *anywhere!*" he barked. *"You stay right here and wait till I get back!"*

She whirled and glared at him. "No."

Though she'd spoken quietly, he wasn't used to her defying him and that one, single word struck him like a slap.

T he Bar D Riders were waiting for him when he finally struggled out onto the porch twenty minutes later. He hated the fact that Prince had to help him mount, but there was no help for it. If the men saw him struggling just to slip one foot into the stirrup, it would make him look even weaker than he was. So he gritted his teeth and let Prince boost him up into the saddle as if it were an everyday occurrence, and then settled himself while Prince swung astride his own animal.

Charlie came out onto the porch, dressed for travel. She called: "Daddy," but Devlin pretended not to hear her.

"Let's ride!" he snapped. He spurred his horse forward, Prince and the men galloping after him.

A lthough he had no way of knowing it, Jonah halted his team in almost the same place that Everett Cooper had stood and watched Sam lead his ever-increasing herd out of the canyon the day before. It was late afternoon and the setting sun was casting long shadows across the high cliffs that surrounded him.

It was impossible to forget that this was Comanche country: Cooper had made sure of that. And though he appeared to be alone, the heavy silence was strangely unnerving. Still, there was no turning back now. For once in his life, Dr Quincy

Martin Jonah was not about to quit, no matter how hard or dangerous the trail ahead became.

He snapped the reins and the horses continued on toward Blanco Canyon.

When he was still some way out, he saw a Comanche war lance stuck in the dirt in the middle of the trail. Even from this distance its meaning was clear.

Stay away!

Jonah pulled up the team and rubbed his jaw uneasily as he stared at the white-red-white, feather-decorated lance. He then took another look around, taking in as much detail as he could. He saw nothing else to cause alarm, but that didn't mean a thing. The Comanches were out there somewhere, he felt sure of it.

Climbing down from the wagon, he went up to the lance. A warm breeze ruffled the feathers. Jonah shivered and then turned his attention to the ground in search of hoof-prints.

The tracks were plain to see. Some fifty horses had left quite a trail behind them. The tracks led into Blanco Canyon. Jonah knew that meant he had to go into Blanco Canyon behind them and again he shivered.

Taking out his flask, he took a long pull of liquid courage. Then he pulled himself back onto the wagon and urged the team forward, around the lance.

Hunkered behind a rock, Lon Cory watched the wagon vanish into Blanco Canyon. Only when it disappeared did he break cover and quickly retrace his steps over a rise to where he had left his horse tied to some scrub. He gathered his reins, toed in, swung up into the saddle and followed the rim toward the canyon.

He hadn't gone more than a quarter-mile when he spotted smoke rising into the blue sky away to the northwest. He drew rein at once. The smoke was dense and dark, broken into puffs that made it obvious he was watching a Comanche smoke signal.

He chewed worriedly the inside of his cheek, torn between turning back and continuing on. He wasn't sure what was worse—running into a pack of scalp-hungry Comanches or being bawled out by Major Devlin for leaving his job half-done.

Edgy now, he looked behind him, froze again when he saw another smoke signal smudging the sky behind him.

He realized he didn't have much choice in the matter. He *had* to go on.

It was then he heard an odd rushing sound that seemed to be coming from someplace behind him. Before he could turn around, a war arrow punched into his back. Crying out in pain, he slumped over and slid from the saddle. He hit the ground hard and his horse shied nervously away from him. Cory squirmed in the hot dirt. Then he shuddered, everything went dark, and he lay still.

Satisfied that the white man was dead, the Comanche crouched on the ledge above him shouldered his bow and jogged off to reclaim his pony and go join his brothers.

The ride took its toll on Devlin, as Prince had known it would. But the stubborn sonofabitch refused to slow the place. He was damned if he'd complain or show any more discomfort than he could help. It wasn't just a matter of pride, it was his old army training coming back to the fore—that you led by example. If you quit before the job was done, it sent a message to your men that it was okay if they quit, too. And Devlin would never allow that. You didn't build the biggest spread in the territory by going easy on yourself or the men you employed. You had to be hard, determined, willing to face any adversity to see things through to the end.

Still, he couldn't deny it; he was aching like hell and fit to drop. Only his hatred for his quarry and what that Zulu bastard had done to him drove him on. But he'd feel better once he'd settled that particular account; he knew he would.

"You can take that look off your face," he growled suddenly.

Prince, riding abreast of him, looked at his profile. "How's that again, Major?"

"You're like a mother hen," Devlin told him, keeping his eyes on the trail ahead. "And I can't say as I like it."

"Well, I'm damned if I'll apologize for caring what happens to you," Prince replied. "We've rode many miles together, Major. With any luck we'll ride a few more yet. But we won't if you keep pushin' yourself this hard."

To his surprise, Devlin said: "You're right, Jim. We *have* come a far piece together. But that doesn't give you the right to question me. You're still the hired man, remember."

Prince's mouth tightened.

"What I do," Devlin continued, "is my affair. So keep your concerns to yourself."

Prince dropped back, not trusting himself to hold his tongue the way he had so often in the past. He'd kept the peace because he had respect for the Major and didn't wish to ruin what little chance he had to be near Charlie. But it was getting harder and harder. Sooner rather than later, he was going to have to make a decision whether to keep taking it or stand up for himself.

The afternoon wore on. He watched Devlin sway in his saddle. Every so often the Major's head would droop, his chin would hit his chest, and then he'd jerk back awake and force himself to ride on. But as the sun began to slide west, even Devlin realized that they could go no farther until the following dawn.

He called a halt and the men gratefully off-saddled, saw to the comfort of their horses and then made small campfires and boiled up beans and coffee. Ever the soldier, Devlin had guards posted and then struggled up to high ground so that he could study their back-trail through an old pair of field glasses he hadn't used since the Battle of Palmito Ranch.

Prince joined him. He knew what the Major was looking for, and saw by the sudden hunching of his boss' shoulders that he'd seen her approaching.

Charlie.

When Devlin lowered the field glasses he was surprised to find Prince staring at him. They looked at each other for a long moment. Then the Major said softly: "I should've known she wouldn't give up."

Prince shrugged. "She's your daughter, Major," he replied simply.

Devlin nodded, sighed. "Bring her in, Jim."

"Yo." He hurried away.

Devlin, too tired and in too much pain to do anything else, could only lean against the rock and watch him go.

Prince mounted up and rode back along the trail. Charlie reined in when she saw him riding toward her. She was as tired as her horse, but pleased to see him. He closed the distance quickly, and tipped his hat politely.

"You all right, Miss Charlie?"

She nodded. "You're going to tell me to turn around and go on back, aren't you?"

"No, ma'am."

"You mean Daddy's actually going to let me ride with you?"

"I don't think he has much choice, do *you?*"

She reflected on that for a moment. Then she smiled warmly at him; warmer than he'd ever seen before.

"I'm glad to see you, Jim."

"The feeling's mutual, Miss Charlie."

Perched atop a craggy column of rock, Sam surveyed the area with *assegai* in hand. The rock jutted out from an almost continuous ridge that walled in one side of the long narrow valley. Twilight had fallen and below Sam the horses grazed and drank peacefully around a waterhole.

As he turned back to the herd, U-Shee-nah started up the slope toward him. As she did so, Red Eye whinnied angrily and quickly moved to block her path. U-Shee-nah stopped, respectful of the albino's bared teeth, but gave a whinny of displeasure.

Sam watched the showdown for a moment. The albino was still challenging his authority, as he had expected him to, but the challenges were becoming less and less frequent as time went by.

Picking up a small rock, the Zulu threw it at Red Eye. It bounced off the albino's neck. More startled than hurt, Red Eye reared up in rage. U-Shee-nah trotted around him, up the slope to Sam.

Thwarted, the stallion shook his head and vented his rage by charging through a nearby group of horses. They quickly scattered.

Red Eye reached the waterhole, stopped and drank ... and once more peace claimed the canyon.

Chapter Twenty-One

Daybreak found Jonah still following the trail the herd had taken. Around him, Blanco Canyon was enveloped in a near-silence that was broken only by the creak and squeak of harness and ungreased wheels. Gradually the ground started to trend downwards at a slight angle as it fed into what Everett Cooper had told him was Mesquite Valley.

Jonah had an uneasy itchy feeling he was being watched all the way in.

When he finally found enough courage to do so, he glanced uneasily to his right and saw them. There was about twenty of them, riding along the ridge that ran parallel to him. They appeared to be disinterested in him, but he wasn't fooled for a moment. They knew he was here, had known it for a long time now, and were shadowing him because it was their idea of fun—to scare the hell out of him so that he'd be good and rattled before they finally came in for the kill.

Cautiously, keeping one eye on them all the while, Jonah reached under the wagon seat and brought out the rifle. He set the weapon across his knees but was disappointed when it failed to give him the comfort he'd been expecting.

As they rode on, he worked up a little spit and tried to whistle, figuring that two could play at this game. If the Comanches heard him whistling like he didn't have a care in the world, they might figure he was crazy and leave him alone. They did that, he'd heard. Trouble was, he realized fearfully, his mouth was so dry he couldn't manage even the softest whistle.

God, I need some whiskey, he thought.

Abruptly the Comanches kicked their horses into a trot and disappeared on the far side of the ridge. Jonah watched them go, wondering what he could expect next. Nothing good, that was for sure.

He looked around, searching for cover, a good place to make a stand. There was plenty of nothing. It was as if the land had been flicked out like a tablecloth, with all the folds smoothed down until there was nothing but endless flats in which even an ant would have had a hard time hiding.

There was a V-shaped split in the ridge ahead. Sometime in the past a rock fall had opened a natural trail that descended to the valley floor. With a jolt, Jonah realized that this was where the Comanches would attack from; that they had vanished from sight so that they could follow a trail down to the split that would give them access to the flats.

Realizing that his only chance was to make a run for it, he yelled at his horses and used the reins to whip them into a gallop.

Even as the ambulance swayed and rattled dangerously fast across the valley, the first of the Comanches descended the rocky trail and came after him, yelling and screaming. He and the others were all painted for war and armed with clubs, lances, bows, and whatever guns they'd been able to kill, steal or trade for.

Jonah slapped the reins harder, but the wagon was heavy and the team built more for stamina than speed. He heard the crack of rifles above the drum of hooves, and bullets began zipping past him. Holding the reins one-handed, he levered a shell into his rifle, pointed the gun back toward the Indians and fired. He didn't expect to hit anything, but hoped the bullets would deter the Comanches and make them realize that he wasn't going to be easy pickings.

He was fumbling to reload when the wagon hit a rock, lurched dangerously and then plunged over onto its side, snapping the tongue and letting the team race on.

Hurled off the seat, Jonah hit the ground hard enough to stun him.

Moments passed, and then he struggled to his hands and knees and looked desperately around for the rifle. Seeing it nearby, he threw himself at it. Bullets and arrows struck the dirt about him. The Comanches were closing fast and Jonah knew he had to be ready for them.

He dived behind the wrecked wagon and opened fire on them. His first bullet caught a pony in the chest and it went down, throwing its rider over its head.

Jonah shot him. But there were still more warriors than he could ever hope to fight off.

Trying not to panic, he continued firing.

Seconds later the first of the Comanches was upon him. The brave's pony leapt over the wagon, its painted rider thrusting his feathered lance at Jonah.

Jonah pumped a shot into him, knocking the savage from his horse. He levered in another round and raised his rifle to shoot the next onrushing Comanche.

But it was then he realized they weren't charging him anymore. Instead they were milling around as if in confusion.

Jonah frowned, wondering what had stopped them.

Then he heard it—a thundering roar that was growing ever louder.

He looked around. And it that moment he saw what had alarmed the Comanches—a vast herd of wild horses came boiling over a nearby ridge, the panicked horses heading straight toward the Indians.

And running beside them, screaming savagely was—

Jonah swallowed.

I'm dead, he thought, *and nobody troubled to tell me. The Comanches killed me and here I am, watching my past life unfold before me.*

Sam—it *was* Sam!—leapt down the slope and hurled his *assegai*. It buried in the chest of one of the Comanches, knocking him from his horse.

Then the herd hit the rest of the Indians full-on.

The startled ponies reared up, tossing their riders beneath the pounding hooves of the stampeding mustangs. Chaos reigned everywhere. Ponies went down, snorting and screaming, throwing off their riders. Other Comanches tried to turn their mounts around to escape the onrushing herd. Some managed it; many didn't.

Jonah watched, open-mouthed, as the charging mustangs trampled over the trapped Comanches. Finally, a great dust cloud hid the slaughter from Jonah.

He heard Comanches screaming and their ponies neighing shrilly. Then Sam burst through the curtain of dust and charged at Jonah, *assegai* reclaimed and held ready to stab.

Watching him come, Jonah thought: *My God, he's going to kill me. He's so mad at me he's saved me from the Comanches so's he can kill me himself!*

Chapter Twenty-Two

B ut Sam stopped before him and made no attempt to stab him with the *assegai*.

Jonah lowered his rifle and looked at the Zulu towering above him.

As always, Sam's expression gave nothing away.

At last Jonah cleared his throat. "I, uh … I don't suppose you could find a little … you know … uh … " he swallowed " … *mercy* … in your heart for a stupid old man?"

Sam didn't say anything.

Jonah arched an eyebrow. "No? Well, I can't say as I blame you, old friend … "

Still the impassive Zulu didn't speak.

But Jonah thought—hoped—that he saw a faint smile stir Sam's lips.

"You lucky I hear sound of battle from afar," the Zulu said finally. He thumbed toward the ridge. "Come take a look."

Jonah beamed. "You're right. I *am* lucky. And grateful, too."

Cautiously he extended his right hand.

After a moment Sam took it.

"Now we even," he said stoically.

All around them things had quietened down. The remaining Comanches had fled. The mustangs milled nervously, waiting for Sam to return to them. U-Shee-nah and Red Eye stood together, appearing almost to oversee the herd.

Jonah ached for a drink, but right now that could wait. Sheepishly he said: "Chief … listen, about the mare. I'm sorry. I was wrong, *way* wrong, and there hasn't been a day that I haven't regretted it. Fact is, that's why I came back, to find you and tell you that—"

Sam stopped him. "It does not matter anymore. U-Shee-nah is Sam's now. All is good."

"Sure, sure. And I'm real happy for you. But … look, Chief, you can't spend the rest of your life with a bunch of horses! You need to be among other humans. No, no, let me finish," he said as Sam started to speak. "What we should do now is head for some place where we're not known—California, say—and start building up our savings again."

Sam shook his head. "Sam stay here, now. In the wild. With U-Shee-nah."

"But that's crazy! You're a human being—you can't live with *horses!* That's—"

He broke off, alarmed, as Red Eye gave a sudden whinny of warning. Sam and Jonah turned just as a bunch of riders off to the west began to cross the valley toward them.

"Damn!" exclaimed Jonah. "Those devils are coming back for more!"

"No," said Sam, shading his eyes. "These are *white* men."

Jonah saw that he was right. They were Bar D riders—and they were coming fast.

"Listen, Chief, you've got to get out of here."

"And you?"

"Forget about me. You're the one they're after. Now, get going. Hurry!"

Sam didn't move. He studied Jonah, long and hard.

"You hear me?" Jonah insisted. "Get going—and *keep* going!"

Sam continued to look at Jonah, seemed to look *into* him, and then said softly: "I will think of you."

Jonah choked on a lump but didn't say anything.

Sam turned and ran to the herd.

"I'll think of you too, Chief … " Jonah murmured thickly.

O

Out in the valley, Devlin saw Sam and the herd escaping up the slope and became enraged. "Shoot him!" he screamed. *"Shoot him!"*

Prince and the other Bar D hands drew rein, pulled out their rifles and opened fire at the Zulu. But the range was too great, and they were cowboys, not marksmen. Sam continued to scramble up the steep slope with horses all around him—until someone got lucky. Sam suddenly stiffened and went down clutching his left thigh.

"I got him!" yelled one of the riders.

But he spoke too soon. Sam struggled to his feet and limped on up the slope. Finally he reached the summit, was silhouetted there for a moment, and then disappeared down the other side.

Relieved, Jonah flopped down on a rock beside his overturned wagon and took a swig from his flask.

Moments later Devlin, Charlie, Prince and the men rode up.

"Get after him!" Devlin bellowed at the riders.

Grudgingly, his men rode off after Sam.

Devlin struggled to dismount. Prince quickly swung down and tried to help him. But the Major pushed him aside and limped painfully up to Jonah.

"I ought to kill you!" he snarled.

Jonah cringed but offered no protest.

Charlie, afraid that her father would carry out his threat, looked at Prince for help.

Prince stepped close to Devlin. "Major, let me handle this."

"Shut up!" Devlin snapped. Then, to Jonah: "On your feet, old man!"

Jonah did as he was told, but not quick enough to suit the rancher. Devlin grabbed him and jerked him up. "See this?" he asked, indicating his disfigured face. "Your man did this to me. This and more!"

Jonah didn't know what to say.

"I'm gonna kill him for that!" Devlin added. "You understand? Hunt him down and—"

He broke off as some of his men rode up. Sam wasn't among them.

"Well?" Devlin demanded.

Hamblin said: "We lost him, Major. There's a hundred different canyons back there, an'—"

"Where're the others?"

"Still lookin'. Rivers seen some blood an' we split up."

"What about the herd?"

"We saw plenty of tracks, but no horses."

"You fool! That many horses can't just disappear!" Devlin turned back to Jonah. "Where the hell is he?"

"I don't know."

Devlin backhanded him. Jonah staggered, but didn't go down.

Charlie looked away, hating what her father was doing and what he'd become.

"You tell me where that black devil's gone or I'll shoot you where you stand!"

"I don't *know!*" Jonah repeated. "Major, I swear—"

Devlin started to draw his six-gun, but Prince stepped in close and snapped: "Hold on, Major! He can't tell us nothin' if he's dead!"

Consumed by hatred now, Devlin had to fight not to pull the trigger. Then he regained control of himself and holstered his Colt. "He's yours!" he told Prince. "Make the bastard talk!"

Charlie said: "Daddy, he just said he—"

"You keep out of this, Charlie!"

Fearfully, Jonah watched as Prince leaned over him, fists clenched. "You heard the Major. Start talking."

"W-Wait a minute, please," Jonah begged.

Hating himself for doing it, Prince grabbed him and backhanded him across the face. "Quit stalling, dammit!"

"I'm not stalling," Jonah said. "I don't *know* where the Chief is. I *swear—"*

Prince belted him. Jonah collapsed on his hands and knees. As he bled onto the dirt, he mumbled: "You can … beat me all you … want. Can even kill me, if you've a mind. But it … won't do you … any good, 'cause I don't … know where the Chief is!"

It was obvious that he was telling the truth. Prince looked at Devlin for instructions. During the beating Devlin's hand had strayed up to his disfigured face. Now it dropped to his six-gun.

Charlie stepped close, her hand closing over her father's. "No, Daddy!"

"Get away, Charlie!"

"Please—don't do it!"

He whirled, out of control now, and slapped her. She staggered back, then recovered, hurt not so much by the blow itself as by the fact that he had actually struck her.

She stared at him for a long, heavy moment. Then:

"You *did,* didn't you?" she blurted, suddenly realizing the truth.

"Did what?" he asked.

"That race … the glass … you *did* order it put there, didn't you?"

Devlin glared at her, not seeming to hear her or see the tears in her eyes, the welt that was reddening her cheek.

Prince stepped forward. *"What's* that?" he asked.

"Major—it's Taylor!" yelled one of the men.

Everyone turned to the rider galloping toward them.

Caked in dirt and sweat, he brought his horse to a stiff-legged halt and slid from the saddle. "We got 'em, Major!"

"Shadow Horse?" Devlin demanded.

"Most likely, yeah. I mean we got the whole herd. Every last head, includin' the mare. Which means Shadow Horse can't be too far away."

Prince said quickly: "He's right, Major. So long as we got the mare, we—"

Ignoring him, Devlin said: "Where are they, Taylor?"

"In a box-canyon, 'bout two miles from here, boss."

Devlin gestured to Jonah and told Prince: "Burn his wagon and bring him along."

Jonah's eyes widened. "No! You can't do that! All I own is—"

"Burn it!"

"No, sir," Prince said softly.

Devlin glared at him. "What was that?"

Keeping his own temper on a tight rein, Prince said: "We're smack in the middle of Comanche country, Major. We burn that wagon, we'll be tellin' every Comanche for fifty miles around that we're here."

Some of the anger faded from Devlin's disfigured face.

"Daddy," Charlie begged, "please listen to him. Jim's right!"

Devlin hesitated, torn, and then nodded. "Put him on a horse and bring him along!" He limped to his own mount. Charlie tried to help him but he pushed her away and though in severe pain, managed to mount unassisted.

Charlie looked at Prince, as if unable to believe this was actually her father.

"Let's go!" Devlin barked and spurred his horse forward.

Chapter Twenty-Three

Where the box canyon was at its narrowest, the Bar D men had built a crude barricade of brush and deadfall logs to corral the herd. As Devlin and the others rode up, Rivers came to meet them.

"They're all in there, Major," said Rivers. "Red Eye, the mare, every last—"

"Any sign of Shadow Horse?"

"No, sir. But he's around here somewhere, Major—can bet on that. He's been hurt, too. I seen blood, 'bout a mile from here—tracked it right into this canyon."

"Could be from one of the horses," said Prince.

"I don't think so, boss. You can see the herd from there. Don't look like none of 'em are hurt."

While Rivers spoke, Devlin studied the high rocky cliffs that surrounded the canyon. "You sure this is the only way out of here?" he asked.

"Real sure, Major. Can see for yourself."

Devlin decided to do just that. He dismounted and limped toward the rocks at one end of the barricade. Prince, Charlie and Rivers tagged along behind. As they walked, Rivers told Prince: "Can't figure out how we missed him, boss. Must've climbed out of here when he seen we got the herd boxed-in."

Prince nodded. But his attention was fixed on Devlin. He watched with a concern shared by Charlie as the Major somehow managed to pull himself up onto the rocks and look at the far end of the canyon. It curved just beyond the barricade then flared out into a vast bowl of land. The herd had gathered against the rear wall. Behind them towered high cliffs.

"So now it becomes a waiting game," the Major muttered. He turned, exhausted and stiff with pain. But when Prince and Charlie made to help him down he snapped: "I can handle it!"

They stepped back, watching silently as Devlin scrambled down with teeth gritted. When he got his wind back, he said: "Wes, you stay. Prince—tell the rest to ride back down the canyon a-ways, and hide among the rocks till they hear my signal—two shots. That'll mean Shadow Horse has broken out the herd. They're to block the canyon and drive it back in this direction ... where I'll take care of Shadow Horse personally."

Prince scowled. "Are you sure?"

"That's an order! Now—help me over to those rocks."

He was referring to some rocks that were in the shade of the cliff overhang, about twenty yards from the barricade. Prince, surprised that Devlin had actually asked for help, gladly provided it.

"What about the old man?" Prince asked.

Devlin glanced back at Jonah, who was standing beside the barricade and looking off toward the rear of the canyon.

"He stays, too," he replied at length. "I want him to see how his friend dies."

Prince drew a breath. He'd had enough of this vendetta and it was clear in his tone. "Major?"

"What is it?"

For another moment Prince held his tongue. Much as he wanted to quit, he was still loyal to this man he had once loved and that loyalty wouldn't let him. There was Charlie, too. If he quit Devlin, he'd never see her again, and he wasn't sure he could stand that.

"Nothin'," he said, and hated himself for backing down again.

Like Devlin, Sam was in pain and damned if he'd show it. He didn't even admit it to himself. But the thigh wound had bled him out and left him weak and light-headed.

He knew, though, there was no time for weakness now. All that mattered was the horses trapped in the box canyon below him, and in particular U-Shee-nah.

As Jonah watched, Red Eye drove the mare back toward the rest of the herd. He then reared up and whinnied with rage at the barricade that held him prisoner. Beyond the barricade, the Bar D riders were preparing to leave. Sam watched them ride out, finding comfort in the fact that the odds against him had just dropped a little.

He looked toward Jonah, standing at the barricade watching the horses. Anger flared when he saw how his friend had been beaten.

He then looked at Prince and Rivers, talking nearby. Devlin and his daughter sat in the shade of the cliff overhang.

He knew Devlin was using U-Shee-nah as bait and knew there was very little he could do about breaking the mare loose. But it was not in him to admit defeat. U-Shee-nah was his, and he was hers. He would risk anything to save her, no matter the odds.

He realized suddenly that the mare was looking right at him. She had sensed him there, knew he had come for her, and all at once she gave a lonely whinny that wrenched at his guts.

What was it Jonah had said? *You're a human being—you can't live with horses!* But as he now understood beyond any doubt, horses were closest thing to a family that he was ever likely to have.

He checked the position of the sun. Soon it would be night. And in the darkness he would do what had to be done.

The campfire had burned to ashes. Around it, everyone appeared to be sleeping in their blankets. Sam watched them for a long time, wondering if Devlin and Prince were only pretending; that they were really just waiting for him to show himself so they could trap *him* as well.

It seemed likely.

One of the figures stirred suddenly. It was Jonah, who had been tied and left several yards from the protection of the overhang. The lone guard, Wes Rivers, was seated on a rock at one end of the barricade with a rifle across his lap. He looked over his shoulder at Jonah and then faced out into the night again.

A low whinny came from the rear of the canyon. Rivers turned, but that was his only movement. His orders had been specific; the Major had made sure of that.

Remember, I want *Shadow Horse to try and break those horses out. So if you hear anything, don't sound the alarm ...*

It was hard, though. Sure, it *could* be Shadow Horse out there. But then again it could just as easily be Comanches. Rivers stirred despite himself. Another whinny only made him feel even more uneasy. And now there were other sounds. The horses were getting restless, starting to shift and trot around.

Beneath his blanket, Jim Prince heard the sounds and his fingers tightened around the rifle he held beside him. He listened intently, heard Devlin breathing fast, excitedly, knew that he was also waiting for the right moment to act.

Sensing the tension, Jonah stopped struggling to loosen his bonds. He craned his neck a little but couldn't see a damned thing in the darkness. But if it *was* Sam out there ...

No, Chief, he thought. *It's a trap. Don't try it!*

He renewed his efforts on the ropes, but they'd been tied expertly. There was no give in them at all.

It took Sam a long time to climb down the canyon wall. Hand- and foot-holds had to used carefully, for not only was Sam struggling with his thigh wound now, but he was working in almost complete darkness. The descent seemed to take forever. By the time he dropped the last few feet to land silently in a crouch, he was sweating hard and the world was spinning around him.

He remained crouched for a while until a wave of nausea passed and he felt capable of pushing on. Rising, keeping his eyes on the barricade, he limped toward the bunched, restless horses.

U-Shee-nah saw him coming and trotted over to meet him, but Red Eye was quick to move into her path and drive her back. The albino then turned to face Sam and did exactly what Sam had known he would—he charged.

But Sam knew something else besides; or hoped he did—that the charge was yet another bluff.

He forced himself to stand his ground as the stallion rushed at him. The stallion galloped closer, closer …

… then stopped.

Man and horse eyed each other warily, the stallion still struggling to get the full measure of his opponent. Then Sam turned away from the horse and started limping toward the barricade.

As the barrier drew closer, Sam dropped onto his belly and snaked the rest of the way in, determined to leave nothing to chance. Forcing himself to move slowly, he edged closer toward the back of Rivers. Seconds later he heard the man sigh with boredom. His breathing seemed normal, regular; if he suspected anything, he wasn't letting it show.

Sam slowly rose up until he was standing directly behind him.

Rivers had no idea the Zulu was there until he struck.

Swiftly, Sam wrapped both arms around Rivers. One hand clamped over his mouth, the other curled around his throat. He yanked the man backwards. Rivers was too startled to offer any resistance. Sam hauled him down behind the barricade, straddled him and punched him in the face. Rivers gave a faint moan and went limp, unconscious and bleeding from the nose.

Chapter Twenty-Four

Sam paused, expecting the alarm to be raised at any moment. It wasn't. At last he straightened up, reached over the barricade and grabbed the rifle Rivers had dropped.

He looked at the sleeping figures. Only one was moving—Jonah. It looked as if he was trying to free himself.

He descended the rocks and limped to the center of the barricade.

Dawn was approaching. He had to work quickly. Setting down the rifle, he began to clear a path through the barricade, hating the extra time he had to take to favor his wound and work as quietly as he could.

Behind him, the nervous horses continued to wander restively.

Sam continued to work until he had cleared a gap in the barricade that was wide enough for the horses to run through. Then he picked up the rifle and trotted back to the herd.

They watched him come, Red Eye out front, intent on challenging him again. But there was no time for confrontation now, so Sam skirted the wary mustang and headed for the western flank of the gathered horses. Red Eye watched him go, prepared for now at least to bide his time.

Sam hobbled around behind the herd. His eyelids were drooping and he was sweating more than his efforts justified. He felt feverish and dizzy, and realized his wound had become infected. But there was nothing he could do about that now. Later, perhaps … if there *was* a later.

Momentarily, his mind wandered, and was startled when he suddenly came back to his senses. Then he pointed the rifle skyward and screamed at the top of his lungs.

"Baleka! Bebeta!"

At the same time he fired the rifle into the air. It bucked wildly in his hands because he wasn't used to the recoil, but by the time he'd loosed off five or six shots he was handling it as if he'd been shooting all his life.

By then the herd had bolted, as he'd hoped it would, the mustangs racing in a long, strung-out line with Red Eye at its head, toward the gap in the barricade.

"Dhlikilili!" Sam yelled.

He tried to run after them, but he was completely spent now. The best he could manage was a shambling trot that would have put his village elders to shame.

D evlin and Prince boiled up out of their blankets, rifles cocked. Prince yelled for Rivers. The absence of reply told him all he needed to know.

Charlie was struggling out of her blankets as well, blonde hair awry. Prince went to her, grabbed her by the arm as the ominous sound of running horses grew steadily louder. He dragged her closer to the overhang, knowing things were going to get dangerous any time now.

"Let go of me!"

"Stay here, dammit!"

Jonah, meanwhile, had struggled to a sitting position and, knowing he was likely to get trampled by the oncoming horses, started yelling: "Help me! Help me!"

Prince looked at Charlie with such determination that she fell quiet. "Stay here!"

He turned and started toward Jonah.

Devlin snapped: "Leave him!"

Prince whirled. "But—!"

"You heard me!"

Seeing mutiny in Prince's expression, he aimed his rifle at Prince's belly. Around them the pounding of hooves grew louder, closer, and the ground shook underfoot.

Prince rebelled—at last.

"Sorry, Major."

He turned to go help Jonah.

Devlin reared back, shocked by his foreman's defiance. On top of everything else, it was too much. He brought the rifle stock to his shoulder, unable to grasp the barrel with his injured hand, having to rest it across the forearm instead.

Even as he drew a bead, Charlie saw what he was going to do and screamed: "Daddy—no!"

But her voice was drowned by the boom of the gun.

Prince grabbed his side, spun, collapsed and lay still.

Instinctively Charlie ran forward, unable to believe that her father had just shot a man who had once meant so much to him, a man that she'd never really cared for until this moment—

Furious, Devlin grabbed her wrist as she passed him, dragged her around and pushed her back into the safety of the overhang.

Before she could do anything else, the first of the stampeding horses—Red Eye—came surging around the bend in the canyon. Right behind him ran U-Shee-nah and all the others, a dam-burst of horseflesh that couldn't be stopped.

Jonah watched them come, wide-eyed and almost paralyzed with fear.

Then self-preservation kicked in and he rolled awkwardly toward the far canyon wall. Over, over, again, again, moving too slowly to have any prayer of getting out of the horses' path—

The ground trembled now and the rumble of horses' hooves filled his ears. He heard Charlie scream—leastways *thought* he did—and when his head snapped around he saw Red Eye bearing down on him and thought: *No ... no ...*

At what seemed like the very last moment the stallion leapt over him and continued running. Jonah couldn't believe his good fortune. But already the next horse was bearing down on him, and even in the poor pre-dawn light he recognized it as U-Shee-nah—

The mare leapt over him as well, and raced on after Red Eye.

Shaking now, feeling as if he was going to vomit at any moment, Jonah continued to roll out of the way of the rest of the herd.

Finally he came up hard against some rocks. Realizing that they would provide a protective nest for him, he scrambled on until he was curled up behind them.

Then he was out of time.

The rest of the herd went blurring past, running shoulder to shoulder, all of them jostling each other for a better position. Dust rose everywhere, choking Jonah. Stones flew up from beneath digging hooves. Panic gripped him. A voice in his mind screamed as he wondered if and when this nightmare was ever going to end.

Then the last of the horses passed him … and it was over—this part of it, at least.

Dazed, Jonah struggled to sit up. He saw Devlin on the far side of the canyon, beside his daughter under the rocky overhang. The sound of the stampede faded, dust began to settle slowly back to earth. And out of the dust came—

Jonah's mouth worked soundlessly.

Chief …

Digging deep, finding reserves he had never until this moment suspected, Sam came jogging out of the canyon behind the horses, the rifle—now empty—held like a club.

Jonah felt the sudden smart of tears in his eyes. Sam looked like a corpse no one had bothered to tell was dead. Jonah's face twisted with emotion and relief. Then he caught a movement out the corner of his eye and when he looked that way, he saw Devlin angrily aiming his rifle at Sam.

Jonah screamed: *"Chief! Look out!"*

He was too late.

Devlin's rifle barked and Sam staggered and dropped to his knees, bleeding from a ragged shoulder wound.

Devlin stared at Sam, consumed by hatred for everything he stood for. He again raised the rifle, ready to finish the Zulu off. Sam braced himself, knowing the man was going to make him suffer before ending his life once and for all.

The bones, Sam thought, watching as Devlin moved closer. *They were right. They said I would die here.*

"Daddy—no!"

Without warning Charlie threw herself at her father, trying to tear the rifle from his hands.

Sam tensed, ready to hurl himself at Devlin.

But Devlin pushed Charlie aside and she fell against the rocks.

Devlin brought the rifle up again, finger whitening on the trigger.

Sam stared defiantly at him.

The blast of gunfire sent echoes through the canyon … but it was Devlin's face that contorted.

He twisted around, one shoulder suddenly bloody, the arm hanging limp and lifeless. He staggered, righted himself, and with extraordinary effort began to slowly, surely raise the rifle again, intending to fire it one-handed.

Before he could fire, Jim Prince was in his face. The wounded foreman's right hand still held the Colt he'd used to wing his employer. Fighting to ignore the pain in his side, he grabbed the long gun from Devlin's grasp and hurled it out into the canyon.

Devlin glared with a mixture of disbelief and fury.

Prince spat his disgust on the ground and went to help Sam.

Hands still bound, Jonah watched as Prince helped Sam to his feet and toward the rocky overhang. In the distance there came a sound like a flashflood, growing steadily louder. It was the Bar D riders driving the herd back, as ordered.

A few moments later the herd appeared around a bend in the canyon. Only Devlin seemed oblivious to them. Obsessed with Sam's destruction, he began to stagger toward his rifle, each step taking him farther from the safety of the rocky overhang.

Jonah yelled a warning. Prince whirled, saw what Devlin was doing, saw that he was walking directly into the path of the oncoming horses—

"Major!"

Devlin ignored him. He continued to stagger toward the rifle. Charlie started after him but Prince grabbed her and dragged her, protesting, out of harm's way.

Devlin's shadow fell across the rifle. He bent, scooped it up, turned back toward the overhang—and now, finally, he seemed to realize what was happening. A great sweep of yellow dust hurled itself along the canyon toward him; a constant, drumming roar grew ever louder in his ears—

He turned and saw them; saw them, and knew there was no escaping them.

His face twisted out of shape and he screamed something inarticulate but somehow defiant, and ignoring the pain in his bullet-broken shoulder he turned back to Sam, used his good arm to prop the rifle's barrel.

It was then the herd slammed into him, sweeping him away so that he vanished beneath roiling dust and pounding hooves.

Charlie screamed and then turned away as the herd trampled over her father.

For several long moments then there was only noise and dust. When that finally faded there was a curious stillness that was broken only by the sound of Charlie weeping.

After the last horses had passed, the Bar D riders reined up, startled by what lay in their path. It was more of a stain than a man and yet they all knew who it was—*had* been.

Rafe Hamblin swung down and hurried over to where Prince still held Charlie, her face buried in his chest as she sobbed and sobbed.

Prince nodded toward Jonah and said: "Untie the old man, Rafe."

Rafe obeyed.

Sam didn't seem to notice them. Moving entirely by instinct, he walked numbly toward U-Shee-nah. The mare stood apart from the cornered herd, watching him. When he reached her he buried his face in her neck and mane. She nuzzled him fondly.

A moment later he collapsed.

Chapter Twenty-Five

It was heading toward midday when Prince and Hamblin boosted Devlin's body up across his saddle with as much reverence as they could and then tied the body tight so it wouldn't slip or fall on the long journey home.

Sam, his wounds now doctored by Jonah and one of the hands who knew a little something about gunshot wounds, watched from a short distance away. Jonah and U-Shee-nah stood beside him, and the herd grazed peacefully behind them. Though still weak, Sam knew he would survive. He hurt, but he had learned to endure pain a long time ago.

At last the Bar D outfit was ready to pull out. Charlie nodded at something Jim Prince—himself having undergone a little of Jonah's crude surgery—told her, and then walked her horse across to them. She looked ghostly pale in the light of the new day, and her blue eyes were sore from crying.

"It probably doesn't mean much, coming from us," Jonah said gently, "but we're sorry about what happened to your father, Miss Devlin. Wish it could have turned out different, for everyone."

Sam nodded soberly. "This should not have happened. Any of it."

Charlie looked at them for a long moment, wanting to tell them that the man who had almost been the death of them hadn't really been her father. Rather, it had been what his injuries had made of him. But that would have been a lie. That man *had* been her father. It was just the degree to which he had been prepared to go to get what he wanted that had changed.

Instead she cleared her throat and said in little more than a whisper: "I'll have the men round up your team animals, repair your wagon and fetch it out to you, doctor."

"Thank you, ma'am. I appreciate it."

"And as for you," she said, turning her attention to Sam. "The mare's yours."

Sam stared at her, not entirely sure he'd heard right.

"I give her to you," she said.

Sam looked a little dazed. He stared off into the middle distance for a while, then looked back at her and said: *"Ungakolwa nangomusa."*

It wasn't a *thank you,* exactly. Typically Zulu, it was more of a suggestion that Charlie do something similarly good and right tomorrow, and the day after, and the day after that until the end of her life.

Charlie didn't say anything more. She couldn't trust herself to. Finally she looked from Jonah to Sam, from Sam to the mare. And then she turned to Prince.

"Let's go home, Jim," she said quietly.

He nodded and they turned their mounts away, the Bar D riders falling in behind them.

Sam and Jonah stood there, watching them file out of the canyon. It was very still after they'd gone, until Jonah said: "Wish you'd change your mind, Chief. We'd do well in California, you and I. Why, in no time at all you'd have enough money to go back to your own people."

Sam cut his gaze away to the horses and said softly: "I *am* with my own people, now."

"Are you saying you don't want to go back home to Africa anymore?"

Sam shook his head. "This is Sam's home now," he intoned. "The bones tell me. And the bones never lie."

"They did once," Jonah reminded him. "They said you were going to die here, remember? And you're not dead yet, my friend. Not even *close."*

"The bones did not lie," Sam said from a deadpan. "They say Sam die here. But did not say *when."*

Jonah studied him for a moment, then grinned, and finally chuckled. He looked up at Sam, knowing they would never see each other again and hating the thought. At length he managed a choked: "So long, Chief." And then, to ease the moment: "'Good night, good night! Parting is such sweet sorrow, that I shall say good night till it be morrow.'"

Sam only stared at him.

"Not an admirer of the Bard, eh? All right. What about, 'The pain of parting is nothing to the joy of meeting again.' Dickens."

Sam smiled.

Jonah reached out and gripped his hand. "Look after yourself, friend Sam."

Sam nodded, then turned and walked over to U-Shee-nah.

Jonah watched him lead the mare along the canyon rim, with the herd following on behind, until at length, all were lost in the glare of high noon.